FINDING SHELTER

A POST-APOCALYPTIC EMP SURVIVAL
THRILLER - THE EMP BOOK 8

RYAN WESTFIELD

1

MAX

Max had been walking alone for a week straight. He'd traveled only at night, walking around dusk and going to sleep a little before sunrise.

He wore a large camping pack, mostly full of food and water, as well as things like extra ammunition, maps, a compass, lighters, and some extra clothing.

He still had his Glock with him. He wore it as he always did in its holster. As he walked, he carried an AR-15 in both hands. Only rarely did he sling it over his back. The world had only gotten nastier, and he didn't like walking without his finger close to the trigger if he could avoid it.

It had been several months since the hordes of desperate people had invaded the campground. Months since Max had led the defense of the camp. Months since Max, Mandy, Georgia and the others had barely survived.

In those months, a lot had happened. They'd started to construct something that really resembled a home, with actual structures that resembled buildings. They'd been able to gather more supplies and had in many ways made their day-to-day lives more comfortable.

In some ways, the world was quieter than it had been. Or at least in their part of the country. Max theorized that the masses of people had really all but died out. They'd done some rudimentary calculations on what percentage of the original populations would be left alive, and the numbers weren't pretty. But, in a way, they were comforting. The fewer people that lived, the less danger Max and the others were in.

Of course, those that were left were the people who knew how to survive. They were the dangerous ones. And, in many cases, the amoral ones, the ones who would do simply anything, no matter what, to keep on breathing.

Those were the sorts of people that Max was worried about coming across. They were the reason that he kept his hands on his long gun as much as he could.

Max and the others had done their best to leave the camp as little as possible. They'd had to leave mostly to forage for supplies, hunt for food, and do some scouting, to make sure nothing terrible was coming their way, no army or horde of desperate and violent people. There'd been some contact with people, travelers mostly, who'd seemed if not trustworthy than at least not immediately violent. From them, Max and the others had heard news of the nation.

It wasn't really news so much as rumors. Rumors that seemed to float around like the wind. There was no way anyone could know what was true, except to sort of try to get a gut feeling about how it all sounded.

There'd been wild tails that had immediately seemed false. Then there'd been stories that had initially seemed false, but kept coming up again and again.

One thing that Max had heard over several months, from several different people who'd seemed more or less honest, was that there was a group of good people who were trying to gather together, looking to bring back stability to the torn-apart nation. Max had heard various things about the group, that they were all former members of the armed services, that they were mere civilians, and that it was a mix of all sorts of different men and women, from various backgrounds.

What seemed common to all the stories was that such a group existed, and that they were looking for new people to join.

Gradually, as the idea of the group's reality formed slowly in Max's head over the passing months, he decided that he liked the idea of it. But when asked by anyone if they'd have any contact with it, Max would just shrug and say that it was better to wait and see what happened. He was by no means a selfish person, but the idea of traveling so far from the community he had worked so hard to create, only to see what was happening with another, well, it just didn't seem like a good idea. It seemed like too big a risk. Too big a sacrifice. And for what? For a gamble.

But then the big news had hit. Mandy was pregnant. With Max's baby, obviously.

Things had gotten pretty serious between Max and Mandy. He'd even proposed to her and they'd had a little somber ceremony. No ring. No dress. Only John to officiate the ceremony. But it had been something.

No one was surprised when Mandy had announced her pregnancy. Max had gotten claps on the back from everyone, but the mood hadn't been completely celebratory. After all, it wasn't like there were cigars to pass around. Or a bar to head down to for a round of drinks. Instead, the future of the world, and the baby's future, seemed like a huge, heavy weight that brought the atmosphere down severely.

After all, what kind of future could Max and Mandy's

baby hope to have? It would grow up in a world completely torn apart, a world of uncertainty and madness, a world where the strongest and most vicious survived and the rest had to cling on or perish.

Max and Mandy had had long talks at night by themselves in their little lean-to, discussing their child's future. It was because of these talks that Max had changed his mind about the group that was forming to the west of them, this group that they kept hearing rumors about.

Max had decided, completely on his own, that if there was anything he could do to ensure that his child grew up in an orderly world, then he was going to do it. And that meant traveling to see if he could help. If there really was a group out there that was interested in forging the nation once again from its own ashes, then Max knew that, for the sake of his future child alone, he needed to do everything he could do to ensure that the group had success.

Max didn't want his kid to grow up in the world the way it was now. The way Max saw it, he could either do that or stay back at the camp, and do his best year after year to protect his kid. Until Max's own time came. And then the kid would be on its own, using what Max had been able to impart.

That wasn't a bad option. In fact, it was what he had mentally resigned himself to for a long while.

But how could he live with himself, if he didn't do everything that he could do to try to actually create order again in the world?

He had heard good things about the group that was forming. Reasonable things. Realistic objectives. Realistic goals.

And the leader? Apparently, there was a leader who was not only charismatic, but wasn't in the least bit a charlatan or a demagogue. He wasn't leading people astray. He wasn't trying to form some kind of cult. He was some kind of ex-cop or ex-military guy. The stories varied sometimes. But what all the stories agreed on was that this man's name was Grant, and that he was about fifty years old.

What Grant wanted to do was start establishing order on a local level. He needed representatives from various areas to travel to him, to discuss the plans, and to establish what would essentially be police-force-type military all around the country. They'd try to make some kind of headway against the mounting violence of the roving bands of absolute criminals who were wreaking so much havoc.

Max would travel there, see whether this leader Grant was the real deal. He'd hear his terms, and if he thought it was all well and good, he'd return to the camp to carry out the plans, whatever they might be.

Max wasn't taking anything at face value. He wasn't that kind of person, and if anything, his experiences since the EMP had proved his natural skepticism to be right on the money most of the time. If anything, he'd learned to be even more careful than he naturally was.

Max planned to spend more time at Grant's camp than strictly necessary. The idea was to hang around and really see if this was something legitimate or whether it was just another man trying to gain power in desperate times by appealing to people's natural desire to improve things.

No one had wanted him to go. His brother had argued with him for days. Georgia had told him it was a terrible idea. Dan, who'd grown to really look up to Max, almost like a son, had said nothing, but Max could easily read the disappointment on his face.

Mandy had been the most convincing. After all, they'd found that they loved each other. She was carrying his baby.

She had the most say of anyone. And she hadn't wanted him to go.

Max's reasoning had been that he wasn't going to be away for that long. It wasn't like he was leaving permanently to join up with some distant militia. He was going to be there for a few weeks. Add on a week of travel at either end, and it was just several weeks really. No more than six, Max had told Mandy.

He'd told her how he was doing it for their child, and she'd asked him how he could possibly leave her while she was pregnant.

It'd been the toughest decision Max had ever made, and he'd told her that. The idea of restoring order, of starting to squash the chaos, was just too big a draw.

Because while there hadn't been many attacks on the camp since the hordes several months ago, and while the masses had for the most part died off, it wasn't as if the world was safe. Far from it. Along with the rumors of Grant and his militia and plan came rumors of other groups forming. Groups of vile men and women. Groups who wanted nothing more than power. Groups of the types of people that society had, before the EMP, hemmed in and tried to control.

Without someone with a plan, without some good people standing up for what was right, the world was only going to get worse. More violence. More chaos. More horrors.

In the end, Mandy had agreed that he go. Better before the baby was born, anyway.

So far on his solo journey, Max had barely seen any sign of any living person. He'd come across some animals, the odd herd of deer, a couple of lone rabbits. Plenty of birds.

He hadn't shot at them. He had enough food, and he didn't want to draw attention to himself.

The moon had been waxing as he walked, so it was only getting brighter at night. It was easy enough to see. But he did, in many ways, crave the sun.

It was cold at night. It didn't matter how many layers he wore. The chill seemed to soak through right to his bones. The only thing that made any difference was keeping up a fast pace. Normally, the sound of his own boots on the ground was the only thing he heard.

It was lonely, left in the dark with just his thoughts. Dark thoughts of what the world might be like for his child if he didn't succeed on his mission. Dark thoughts of what might happen to Mandy if the world kept turning the way it was turning. He couldn't shake the horror stories that had floated over to their camp along with the other rumors. Stories of people who ruled through fear and torture. People who had sick minds. People who had been, in some way, cast aside or slighted by the pre-EMP society, and who now found an opportunity to seek their revenge on those they believed had harmed them and held them back.

Max was exhausted from a full night of hiking. His leg was hurting him, and he'd been popping aspirin at four-hour intervals to help keep the pain from becoming unbearable.

Dawn had already hit.

Max should have stopped an hour ago. But he'd wanted to push on. He'd barely noticed the light starting to creep up around him.

The sun wasn't yet up in the sky, but the world was once again illuminated.

It had rained off and on throughout the night, and Max

was wet, not to mention sweaty. And getting a little over-heated from the walking.

And he had a lot to do before he went to sleep. He needed to look over his maps. If he'd calculated things right, he should be only a day away from Grant's camp. That meant that he had to strategize more, think things over. He didn't just want to walk in there without his plan fully formed. Of course, he'd been thinking his plan over since he'd left Mandy and the others. But there were always last-minute details to hammer out. He needed time. Time sitting down with a pen and paper and a map.

Sometimes it helped to write things out. Sometimes it helped to see the map in front of him, no matter how much of it he had committed to memory.

The long nights of exhaustive walking made it harder for him to visualize things like the map in his mind's eye. Not to mention harder to think clearly without writing down the ideas.

All night, Max had been walking along a little two-lane country road. He'd been staying about ten feet off of the shoulder, walking near the tree line.

There'd hardly been anything at all. Just the occasional abandoned gas station. The occasional little run-down country house.

And he wasn't expecting to see much more until he arrived at Grant's camp.

But what he saw now made him stop dead in his tracks.

His finger reflexively went inside the trigger guard, pressing ever so slightly against the trigger.

Up ahead, down the wet road, there was an old Jeep parked horizontally across the road. A car could have driven around it, but it would have had to get very close to the Jeep, not to mention drive partially off the road.

Max guessed that there was a good reason someone wouldn't want to get their vehicle very close to that Jeep.

It wasn't there by accident. It looked purposefully placed. It was a strategically advantageous location, right at a bend in the road, with the trees particularly close to the road and nothing else around for at least a mile in either direction.

No one appeared to be there. But Max knew someone was. Probably more than one person.

Max stayed as still as he could. He'd have rather been on the ground, but he knew that if he moved he'd be more likely to be seen.

Possibilities raced through his head.

Who'd put that Jeep there?

Was it Grant and his men? Maybe their project was bigger than Max had expected, with bigger boundaries? Was this Jeep an outpost of a well-ordered militia camp, or was it something else entirely?

It may very well could just be a couple of murderous rogue bandits, waiting for their next victim?

If that was the case, Max didn't have any intention of going down easy.

2

SADIE

Sadie's mother was asleep in her little lean-to. She'd been up for most of the night, keeping watch over the camp. She'd come in to wake Sadie up, passing her a half-full Thermos of coffee that she'd used herself during the watch.

No matter what, Georgia never let Sadie or James sleep in. As she always said, there were always chores to do. Georgia, or Max for that matter, didn't tolerate healthy kids just sitting around doing nothing.

Dan, the only other "kid" around, didn't need to be told things like that. He never needed to be woken up, and he never needed to be told to gather firewood. He was always on top of it all himself, always looking for some way he could help, some way, no matter how small, he could contribute.

In a way, it was annoying. But it wasn't like Sadie and James were any slouches themselves. Sadie's own attitude had changed considerably. She felt as if she was a different person. In fact, if she could have met the version of herself from before the EMP, she would have been annoyed with herself, annoyed at her own spoiled attitude.

Before the EMP, she'd taken everything for granted. And now? She was thrilled to get a Thermos full of leftover coffee from her mother's shift.

Before the EMP, she wouldn't even have liked smelling the coffee. It had just seemed like some gross adult drink to her. But now she joined just about everyone else at the camp in drinking coffee throughout the day.

Sadie couldn't remember exactly who, but someone had come across a huge store of instant coffee on one of the supply-getting expeditions. There was enough coffee that they could all drink a few cups a day for the next couple years.

Sadie felt the coffee's warmth spread through her.

She was sitting on a little rock by herself at the edge of the camp. Everyone was busy. Either sleeping, like her mother, if they'd had a night shift, or they were already working on some project or chore.

James and Dan, who'd become inseparable friends since Dan's arrival at the camp, were hunkered down over a little fire they'd made, eating their breakfast, and making their plans for the day. No doubt, Dan had some new project cooked up in his mind that he was briefing James on.

Sadie had already eaten, and she was feeling a little jealous of James's friendship with Dan.

She still missed her friends from school, back before the EMP. Now that things had been a little calmer in the last several months, there'd been more time to think about those friends and what had happened to them.

Her mother had advised her, in her usual somewhat brusque way, that more than likely her friends were already dead. Her mother didn't believe in sugarcoating things or making them more palatable. She fully believed, as did the other adults at the camp, that James, Sadie, and Dan would be at a huge disservice if truths were hidden from them, no matter how ugly they were.

And it would have been almost impossible for Sadie to not understand the reality of the situation. After all, she'd been through it all with everyone else. She'd been shot at and almost killed. She'd shot and killed people herself. She'd killed adults who, before the EMP, might have been politicians, teachers, policemen, stockbrokers, insurance salesmen, or anything at all.

People had gone crazy. That was Sadie's takeaway from the whole situation.

Unlike the adults, she knew that she was going to grow up and become an adult in this world of chaos and violence. She had a different perspective than the adults did. And, unlike them, she would soon gradually forget the peaceful pre-EMP world of her childhood. The new reality would, for her, become the only reality. Everything else would be just a distant memory.

Sadie still vividly remembered when the hordes of the insane, crazed, desperate people had invaded. She could still see their faces and hear their screams. In contrast, the memory of sitting in the cold, boring classrooms before the EMP were fading rapidly.

The previous few months had been relatively calm. Those strangers who had stumbled upon the camp had been friendly, or at least not violent and dangerous. They'd exchanged news with the adults, traded the odd supply here and there, and continued on their way.

Food wasn't much of an issue, and everyone was eating pretty well. Plenty of calories. Plenty of protein.

There was plenty of venison. Her mother was responsible for providing most of it.

And there were a lot of canned and packaged foods. Taken, mostly, from the surrounding areas on the expeditions that the adults would take.

Max had explained how, in terms of food and pre-EMP world supplies, they were right now in something of a "sweet spot." What he meant was that while there were a limited number of pre-EMP products left in the world, at this point so many people had died off that there were a limited number of "consumers" left. Of course, eventually, all the products that had been found would be consumed, and there'd be nothing left. But for the moment, it wasn't that hard to take a short expedition to some nearby out-of-the-way store that hadn't been hit by the mobs and find some supplies.

There were fewer people out than before, which made such trips possible. But, of course, many of the people left were exceedingly vicious, not to mention dangerous.

A big issue with the food was that they were still relying heavily on packaged foods from the pre-EMP world. And those products would never again be produced. Max had wanted to get farm animals. He'd wanted them to have their own continuous supply of milk, eggs, and eventually meat. But they hadn't yet gotten that far. The few expeditions they'd taken to farms had turned out nothing but dead farm animals. The people who'd cared for and fed the animals had long since died, leaving the animals to either starve or escape. Most of them had starved.

They couldn't rely on venison as their only food. Something might happen to the deer. Someone else might hunt the populations down. Or who knew what else. They'd come to expect the unexpected. Which was why Max wanted their own reliable food supply.

Not to mention the fact that it was dangerous for Sadie's mother to keep heading out on her own on her hunting trips. Sometimes she took others with her, but in general they were needed back at camp for some project or another, like helping build a shelter, construct a fence, or to work on the drinking water systems or toilets.

Everyone knew that however "peaceful" the current times seemed; it was still exceedingly dangerous to venture away from the camp.

Sadie herself was under strict orders never to leave alone. In fact, she hadn't gotten to leave at all since they'd gotten there.

From where she was sitting, she glanced again at James and Dan. They had a map out in front of them now and they were peering at it intensely. On more than a couple occasions, they'd both been allowed to leave together. They'd hadn't gone very far, but they'd gotten to do something important, scout out a potential site for burying backup supplies.

Sadie was jealous. Jealous of their friendship. And jealous of their little useful expeditions. No doubt they were planning another one now, although she could barely hear their voices.

Sadie took another sip of the coffee, and her thoughts turned to the man who'd come by two weeks ago. He'd been in his fifties, with a weather-beaten face and a long, unruly beard. On his watch, Max had found him wandering around the outskirts of the campsite. Max had confronted him, and they'd had a brief standoff, each of them pointing a gun at the other. The man, who'd given his name as Holstead, had agreed to surrender his weapon.

After a long talk, during which time Max had decided the man wasn't a threat, he'd brought him back to the camp, and they'd all sat around the campfire late into the night, discussing the world, the EMP, and trading bits of news.

Holstead had confirmed what others had said about Grant and his militia. Of course, Holstead hadn't seen any of it with his own eyes, but he'd heard it from others.

Holstead had told them about a family that was living not that far away from them. He'd stayed the night at their house, after having an encounter similar to the one he's had with Max. Encounters like that were getting more and more common. And at the same time, encounters where everyone shot first, to kill, were getting more common as well.

Holstead had said it was a little family of three. A mother, a father, and a daughter, who was about Sadie's age. Sadie could still picture Holstead pointing at her as he'd explained the daughter's age.

That family was supposed to be only a couple miles away, in a little house on a little road without many other houses. They were just outside the official park boundaries, and apparently the house was tucked out of the way enough that they'd avoided trouble, for the most part. It was a relatively peaceful area. The mob hadn't gotten them, and the marauders and murderers and thieves hadn't gotten them either.

Sadie glanced again at James and Dan. She felt the jealousy rising in her, coming up from her stomach.

She wanted a friend of her own. She thought of the friends from school who were likely dead.

It wasn't fair. Why did her brother get to have a friend? After all, Sadie had to spend all day with the adults. And they weren't bad, but they could get a little tiresome. Max, for instance, was always barking orders at everyone.

Despite how responsible Sadie had become, she still sometimes felt like she just wanted to goof off. And it wasn't really possible to goof off in the camp, not with all those adults breathing down her neck, telling her to do this or that, until the point where she was tired to the bone and simply needed to eat and sleep.

But if she could find another girl her age, maybe she could goof off a little. Have some fun. Play the kinds of games her mom had told her about, the kinds of games kids used to play before cell phones and computers, the kinds of games that Sadie had only rarely played in her own childhood. Stuff like kicking a ball around. Or tic-tac-toe.

Sadie knew that Dan wouldn't even think about playing a game. He was basically like an adult himself. And James? He'd just laugh at her and tell her to go do something useful.

Sadie glanced around. Everyone was busy. Her mother was asleep.

If she wanted to leave the camp, she could do it now. Easily. John and Cynthia were on watch now, and Sadie knew just how to avoid them.

It was a split-second decision.

She set her Thermos down on the ground, stood up, and quickly made her way away from her brother and Dan.

She moved quickly through the trees, a smile growing on her face.

She couldn't remember the last time she'd smiled like that. Or the last time that she'd felt that she would soon be having some fun.

It didn't occur to her that the girl her age might not even be someone that she'd like or be friends with. After all, one couldn't be that particular in times like these.

Sadie didn't have much with her. Just the basic kit that Max and Georgia had always agreed that every member of the camp needed to have on themselves. Just in case something happened.

The kit had grown over the months, as they'd gathered more supplies.

Currently, the kit included some kind of fire starter, a handgun, ammunition, a knife, and a small bottle of water.

The kit wasn't perfect, but it would take care of the biggest threats to life. Hopefully.

Everyone carried their kit in different ways. Some could stuff it all in their pockets. Sadie's clothes, which were quickly becoming very worn out, often didn't have any pockets, or, if they did, they weren't big enough. So someone had found her a little backpack that she had to wear around all the time.

The little backpack had a cartoon image on it. It was designed for a kid. And its contents now belied the cute images.

The little backpack bounced as Sadie walked through the woods.

They were fortunate enough that there really wasn't a lack of gear. For one thing, there were a few weeks when they could simply walk down the road and find a string of corpses. People who'd died from starvation or violence. And they'd always had something on them. Some piece of gear. Often a firearm or a knife.

Of course, Sadie had just heard all this. She hadn't left the camp since they'd gotten there.

She felt more energized with each step she took. She couldn't wait to meet her new friend. Not to mention just get out of the camp. Away from that stifling atmosphere. And from all that work.

It had rained a little last night, but the sun was now appearing above the trees.

Sadie had the feeling that this was going to be a good day.

She did a mental check on the sun's position, just as her mother had taught her. She needed to make sure that she was headed in the right direction. She needed to make sure she could find that family with the girl about her age.

It took Sadie about an hour to walk to the edge of the national park. She saw no one on her walk. And she saw nothing except nature.

When she'd left the camp, she'd headed in the direction away from the burial grounds, where they'd buried the corpses from the mob. And the others.

Up ahead, there was a small squat building. Some kind of welcome center. Sadie had seen things like that before. It was the kind of place that had a couple of maps pinned up in glass cases. And maybe a couple of restrooms that were locked, no matter what the season.

Off behind the small squat building, Sadie could see the road. It started out as a dirt road, but she could see where it turned into pavement and left the park.

Sadie paused, standing in place. Her hands were on her backpack straps, holding them as if she were headed off to school.

She took a deep breath.

She hadn't left the camp, not to mention the park itself, in so long. Maybe this wasn't such a good idea.

Would the others worry? Surely they'd notice soon enough that she was missing.

And she hated to think that her mother would wake up and not know where she was.

Sadie hesitated, almost turning on her heel and marching back to camp.

But then she thought about it more and realized that no

one had been paying her much attention anyway back at camp. It'd probably take them all day to notice.

And her mother would be asleep almost all day. At least until late afternoon. She'd had a long shift that night, and she'd been hard at work the day before, so she'd need all the sleep she could get.

Sadie thought about it and decided that she'd be able to get back either before her mother woke up, or right after it.

It'd all work out. The adults were just worrying too much about things. Sadie knew that the world was safer now. The adults had admitted it themselves, saying that so many people had died off that the dangers were diminished.

But, even so, Sadie wasn't about to enter the outside world without a gun in her hand.

She may have been young but she wasn't crazy.

Sadie got one arm out of the backpack. Slung the pack around to her front. Unzipped it, and dug in, reaching for the handgun safely stored in its holster.

She got it out. Got her backpack back on both shoulders.

The gun felt good in her hand. A little heavy. But she'd gotten used to it over the last few months.

She liked having her own gun. It meant safety. It meant protection.

And now she was gaining a little independence too.

She'd be back at camp before anyone got worried. It'd all work out.

E veryone went by their last names at the camp. Including Wilson and Grant. It gave the camp a vaguely military feel.

Wilson was seated at his folding card table in his tent. He was going over the clipboards full of paperwork, trying to patch a hole in one of the supply chains. In the past, this kind of work would have been made easier with computers. But, with a little patience, a pencil and paper still did the trick.

Wilson's tent was a large camping tent, the cheap kind that families buy when they know they're only going to be using it once or twice a year.

There were better tents at the encampment. Real camping tents. Tents with even more space. Tents that didn't have tears in the sides and holes in the bottom.

But Wilson had never been the sort of man who had craved luxury. He'd never been the type to try to one-up his neighbors. He was always more or less content with the possessions he had, so long as they were practical.

He cared more about whether something worked than

how it looked. Unfortunately, the same couldn't be said for everyone in the militia. As far as Wilson was concerned, this was wrong. After all, it was a militia, not a summer camp. And, what's more, the world was different now.

But despite the chaos of the world, and the mission they were trying to accomplish here at Grant's camp, there were men who weren't satisfied unless their tents were the best around, their boots new, and their clothes free of rips, tears, and stains.

Wilson was different.

Even before the EMP, Wilson had cared about ideas. About goals. Objectives. About what he was doing in the world.

Nothing had changed since the EMP.

Before the EMP, Wilson had been a high-powered lawyer. He'd always fought the good fight. Pro bono cases, and things he really believed in were his specialty.

He'd been the sort of lawyer who'd made half a million a year easy, and that was with him not even chasing the money the way plenty of his colleagues did.

He'd been respected as lawyer. Very respected. Colleagues constantly consulted him, and international organizations had always been pestering him to give talks at conferences.

He'd always showed up at the conferences in his old scuffed shoes and wrinkled suits. As far as Wilson was concerned, his job required a suit, and that was as far as he was obligated to take it. For him, the job he was doing was more important than his appearance. Everyone already recognized his talents.

The post EMP world was no different. After Wilson had gotten hooked up with Grant, it hadn't taken long for others to recognize his talents. Of course, the work here was quite a bit different than it had been before the EMP. But the ideas were the same. The requirements were similar. Organizational skills were crucial. As were people skills.

The way it stood now, Wilson was something like the personal secretary to Grant, the enigmatic and sometimes mysterious leader of the military camp.

He was nothing like a secretary in the pre-EMP sense of the world. He didn't do much paper shuffling or filing. There were no phones to answer, although sometimes walkie-talkies and various types of radios were used, especially for certain missions.

Wilson's own understanding of Grant was still growing. And now he understood that, if anything, Grant was really more of a politician than anything else. Well, a politician and a thinker as well.

Not many others understood Grant as well as Wilson. And that was because no one had as much personal contact with Grant as Wilson did.

It was Wilson who delivered Grant the daily briefs. It was Wilson who acted as the liaison between Grant and the rest of the militia camp. It was Wilson who plotted with Grant late into the night, trying to find the solution to some particularly difficult organizational problem.

Wilson truly believed in Grant and his mission. He wouldn't have done it if he hadn't.

If Wilson didn't care about restoring order to the country, he would have been off doing something else. Most likely trying to carve out a comfortable lifestyle for himself. There were plenty of others doing it among the wreckage of the country. There were plenty of others who were just starting to get comfortable. Wilson got reports on them all the time.

Wilson couldn't have done what Grant did. There was

just no way. Grant had that charisma. He could walk out of his tent right now and people would just start following him around. Trying to talk to him. Trying to understand what he was thinking.

Sure, a lot of that had to do with the fact that there wasn't a single person in the camp who didn't recognize Grant on sight. But Wilson suspected that it was just who Grant was. He'd always been like that. Even before starting the camp. Just one of those magnetic people. No matter what they did, people were interested. No matter what they said, people listened.

Fortunately, Grant happened to have good ideas. Brilliant ideas.

Wilson was as fully committed to them as Grant was.

Bringing back order to the US? Completely squashing the incredible chaos and violence that had wrecked the nation since the EMP? It almost sounded too good to be true.

But that's where the plan came in.

It was systematic.

It was novel.

It was unique.

It was simple.

It was brilliant, no matter which way you looked at it.

A sudden noise outside Wilson's tent door interrupted his train of thinking.

It was someone clearing their throat. There wasn't any way to really knock on a flimsy tent door, so a lot of the men and women would clear their throats instead.

For some reason, the noise had always annoyed Wilson.

"What is it?" said Wilson, his voice clearly conveying his annoyance.

"Sorry to interrupt, sir," said the man, without continuing. Wilson didn't immediately recognize the voice.

"Just get on with it. Come on in."

The tent flap moved aside, and a short, stocky man entered. Wilson recognized his face, but he couldn't recall his name at the moment.

The man entered awkwardly and moved to where he stood in front of Wilson's table.

Apparently, he saw no need to state his name.

Wilson glared at the man. "Well," he said. "Spit it out. What is it?"

"Ah, yes," sputtered the man, who was apparently nervous as well as awkward. He moved his mouth around for a few moments awkwardly, without any sound coming out. Finally, something seemed to spark in his eye, and he spit it all out. "One of the eastern outposts picked up a man," he said. "They told me to report it to you."

"Picked up a man?" said Wilson. "Well, that's hardly news. What was he doing? Why was he picked up?"

"He'd heard about the movement, sir. He'd heard about Grant. He wanted to join up."

"So?" said Wilson, growing more annoyed by the minute. "I don't see how any of this is news. We have new recruits coming in every day. They've heard the news. They've heard about what we're doing, either from gossip or from the fliers. Why wasn't he taken to the barracks for new recruits? Why are you telling me about this all?"

"He refused to go, sir."

"Refused to go?"

"He's stubborn, sir. Wanted to talk to Grant himself."

Wilson let out a dry laugh. Grant wasn't known for giving audiences to complete unknowns. Especially not people picked up by an outpost or a patrol. "I don't think that's going to happen," said Wilson.

"Well, sir, he's making things quite difficult."

"Is he now?"

The man nodded. There was fear in his eyes, which were darting around nervously. Fear that wasn't just for Wilson and his position. Was it fear for this audacious stranger?

"Send him in. I'll talk to him."

The man nodded and stepped once again through the tent flap.

Wilson sighed as he watched the man go. This, unfortunately, was a large part of his job. He had to smooth out the wrinkles in the camp so that Grant could occupy himself with more important things.

In mere moments, the man returned, this time with another man. Had he been standing outside the tent door all this time?

It was all highly irregular. A new recruit allowed to go as he pleased throughout the camp, waiting outside Wilson's office.

Wilson studied the man. He walked with a slight limp. He was a little taller than average, and of medium build. Carried some muscle, but not a lot. Fairly thin, as most people were these days.

There was an intense look on his face. At least a week's worth of thick stubble.

There was an intense intelligence in his eyes. An intelligence that Wilson didn't see often.

The man carried himself like he was someone. Like he didn't have anything to prove.

He had a commanding presence.

In a way, he reminded Wilson of Grant.

But there was no one like Grant except Grant himself.

"Name?" said Wilson, deciding to discuss the irregularities later.

"Max," said the man.

"We go by last names here, generally."

"Let's just leave it at Max. Are you Grant?"

"Nope," said Wilson. "But I'm as close as you're going to get to Grant today. You're lucky to be talking to me."

"Well," said Max. "That's fine. I just wasn't getting anywhere with your lackey here." He nodded his head to indicate the nameless man who'd brought Max in. "I knew I needed to move up the chain of command."

Wilson had seen this sort of thing before. It was a test. He was trying to see if using the word "lackey" would made anyone angry. Anger was a good way to test a man. Not to mention an organization.

Wilson wasn't falling for the bait. He'd hear this man out, whatever it was he wanted to say. It was all highly unusual. But, then again, Grant himself was in many ways highly unusual. And there was just something about this Max. Something about his presence. Maybe he really did have something to offer. Something unique.

"So spit it out," said Wilson.

"I heard you're looking for local militia leaders," said Max. "I'm here to volunteer, provided everything is up to my standards."

Wilson's jaw dropped. "So you're coming here, a complete unknown, demanding a leadership position."

Max nodded. "That's right," he said. No hint of a smile on his face. His face was dead serious.

"What makes you think we'd do that?"

Max shrugged. "I have the necessary skill set. And I heard you were looking for leaders."

Wilson said nothing for a few moments, his eyes not leaving Max's face.

This was completely ridiculous. Completely absurd. A complete waste of time. He'd been duped, apparently, by Max's "presence," whatever that was. But he wasn't taking any more of it. He had things to do. Important things.

Wilson was getting more annoyed by the second.

"All right," he said, taking his eyes off Max's. "Enough's enough. Throw him in the stockade with the others. I've had enough of this."

"Yes, sir," snapped the lackey, whose name Wilson still couldn't remember.

Max said nothing.

"Come on, buddy," said the lackey, grabbing Max forcefully.

Max didn't resist, but he didn't go willingly either. He just stood there.

In an instant, the lackey had his sidearm drawn and pushed into Max's side.

"You don't have any cuffs?" said Wilson to the lackey.

The lackey shook his head.

"Let me see if I have some."

Underneath the folding card table desk there were a couple crates packed with odds and ends. After a moment of rummaging through one of them, Wilson came up with a pair of plastic binders that functioned as handcuffs. Likely they'd been scavenged from a police station.

Wilson grabbed the binders and tossed them to the lackey, who, without hesitation, snapped them onto Max's wrists.

"Maybe we can talk again," said Wilson. "After the stockades have taken some of the arrogance out of you."

Max said nothing, but he stared Wilson down as he was led out of the tent, cuffed, at gunpoint.

Good. That was how the camp was supposed to run. Efficiently. No nonsense. People with crazy ideas got sent to the stockade. People causing problems got locked up. There was too much to do to get bogged down in the nonsense ideas of every crazy individual who came by.

Now that the nonsense was over, Wilson could finally get back to work. He grabbed a couple of his clipboards and stared at them. But he couldn't quite get himself to focus on the work.

There was something about that man, about Max, that stuck with him. Something strange.

4

TERRY

Terry was headed back home from a scavenging mission. He was weary. His legs were aching. He'd walked too far.

He'd gotten too thin over the last few months, and it felt like his whole body was deteriorating. He wasn't just losing fat, but muscle too. And he imagined that his lymph tissue and thymus was slowly deteriorating as well.

Terry had been studying to be a nurse practitioner before the EMP. He'd taken enough anatomy and physiology classes to fully understand the effects starvation were having on his body.

His joints ached. It felt as if he had arthritis. The symptoms matched completely with what he remembered reading in his textbooks. But he wasn't a day over thirty years old. Likely, it'd been brought on by starvation and stress that had wrecked his hormones.

It was almost like mental torture, knowing exactly what hormones were likely out of whack. He knew exactly why he and his family were suffering. But he couldn't do anything about it.

He felt weak. He felt powerless. He felt that, as the man of the family, he should have been providing for his wife and his young daughter.

And the fact that he couldn't help them tortured him more than the physical agony of the arthritic joint pain. It was almost too much to take, seeing them deteriorate along with himself each day.

He would have done anything for his wife and daughter. Anything. He would have gladly sacrificed himself if it would have meant that they'd be happy, healthy, and safe.

But sacrificing himself would do no good.

His wife was getting weaker by the day. And she'd never had a strong constitution. She couldn't go out and scavenge like Terry could. She wouldn't be able to care for their daughter if something happened to him.

And his daughter? She was too young to be self-sufficient. Far too young.

Terry's resentment and anger were growing stronger by the day. He'd managed to keep his family alive for so long with his intellect. And now? His intellect wasn't failing him, but it was no longer doing him as much good as it'd done in the past.

He was running up against real-world problems that no amount of cleverness could solve. It seemed as if each time he went out on a scavenging mission, looking for goods manufactured by the pre-EMP world, he came up empty-handed.

Before that group had moved into the state park nearby, Terry hadn't had the same kind of difficulties in his scavenging expeditions. He'd known just where to go. He'd known what to expect in terms of confrontations.

But since that large group had come by, the supplies in

nearby stores and homes had been dwindling at a depressing rate.

At least that's the way it seemed to Terry.

Soon enough, there wouldn't be anything left. And Terry and his family would fade away. Either they'd starve to death or their immune systems would weaken to the point where they'd succumb to some infection in the coming winter. Probably pneumonia. The other possibility was that they'd be too weak to defend themselves against some coming attack.

So far, Terry had relied more on stealth than combat. Sure, he carried a gun. A couple of them. He'd taught himself to shoot after the EMP, even though he'd never been a "gun person" before.

Terry had kept this family alive merely with his wits. Others used their strength.

Terry had been strong enough before the EMP. He'd done his cardio and his light weights at the gym. But now? He was weak. And only getting weaker.

His wife wasn't doing well. She was too thin. Far too thin. And right before the EMP had hit, she'd been looking good. Putting on weight nicely to go along with the new pregnancy. And then? She'd had a miscarriage. It had either been the stress or the lack of food. Probably the stress though.

So that dream was gone. The dream of having another kid. A sibling for Lilly to play with. But bringing another child into the world wouldn't have been good.

Lilly wasn't doing so good either. Neither he nor his wife wanted to admit that their daughter would, more likely than not, die. Sooner or later. Unless she got better nutrition.

The way Terry saw it, he'd done everything he could. He'd kept them alive by hiding them in a small section of the attic, behind a false wall. They'd spent days cowering there, with hardly any room to move. They hadn't been able to make any noise. They hadn't been able to do anything, even go to the bathroom properly. They'd had to urinate and defecate while wearing their clothes.

It'd been horrible and humiliating. But they were still alive. The men who'd invaded their home had eventually gotten bored and moved on, leaving behind a wreck of a house.

Terry was getting more tired the more he walked. He still had a ways to go to get home. With each step he took, the more agitated his mind got.

It felt as if his mind was jumping all over the place. He couldn't really keep his thoughts straight. It felt almost as if he was cycling through the same confused thoughts over and over again.

The only thought that he could keep straight was the thought that it all wasn't fair.

It was the thought that told him that there was someone to blame for all this.

Not someone far away. Not whoever or whatever was responsible for the EMP. Not society at large for not creating the proper checks and balances and redundancy systems.

Not himself for not being more prepared.

No. It was all the fault of that group that had moved into the state park nearby. They were sapping the surrounding area of supplies. Soon there'd be nothing left. And that large group would flourish with the help of all those calories.

Meanwhile, Terry and his family would just die off.

Terry was getting angry. His face felt hot. It was probably getting bright red too.

He was walking faster than he normally did. His ratty,

torn-up sneakers were stomping along the ground harder than they normally did.

Each step felt like it might help release his anger. It was if he were slamming his feet against the earth. As if he were trying to punish the entire planet for what it had done to him, for the situation that he was in.

And in that moment, in his intense anger, he couldn't remember that everyone else in the country, and probably the world, was in the same situation. Instead, it felt like he, Terry, was alone in his misery and plight. It felt like he alone were up against completely unfair and unjust odds.

Unless he did something drastic, he realized in his anger, his situation would only deteriorate. He'd only get screwed over again and again until he was dead. And was that fair to his wife and daughter?

No, it wasn't fair that they were stuck with a provider who couldn't even manage to provide.

Terry wasn't paying much attention to where he was headed.

He was walking through the trees blindly, heading in the right direction, but not looking at the ground at all.

Suddenly, his right shoe collided with a small log. He stumbled, and then fell heavily to the ground.

He managed to break his fall partially with his left hand.

But it wasn't quite enough. Pain flared through his weak, arthritic body.

He lay there on the ground, panting. He felt too weak to utter the curses than ran through his mind.

His whole body felt like a disaster. And mentally, he was even in worse shape.

He didn't know if he had the strength to get up. So he just lay there.

He knew that if it weren't for his wife and daughter, he

most certainly wouldn't have the slightest shred of strength. If it weren't for them, he'd just lie there until he died of dehydration. Or until someone came along and put him out of his misery.

It would have been a tough way to go. But it would have been a blessing. He would have welcomed it.

Suddenly, he became disgusted with himself. Disgusted with his thoughts. Disgusted with the idea that he wanted a way out. That he wished he didn't have a wife and daughter.

After all, what kind of man was he? Who wished to die because it was easier?

Well, he was weak.

Terry was weak and he knew it.

But he also knew that he'd eventually get himself off the ground somehow. That he'd find some way to scrape by another day. Find some more half-rotten food somewhere and feed it with tears in his eyes to his family.

Suddenly, Terry heard a noise that sounded like faint footsteps off in the distance.

He wasn't sure if it was just his imagination or not, so he tried to hold his breath, so that his out-of-breath panting wouldn't get in the way of hearing what was there.

Sure enough, there it was. Faint, yes. But definitely there.

Terry moved himself around like a worm, getting into a position where he was lying face down on his belly.

He wanted to be out of view for whoever was coming.

He poked his head up a little to look around.

No sign of anyone.

Not yet.

He waited for a full minute, counting from one to sixty in his head, before poking his head up again.

This time, he saw it.

A person.

But it wasn't the type of person that he was expecting to see.

It wasn't some tall thin man, with scraggly hair and a long, dirty beard. Sometimes, it seemed as if those were the only types of people he came across these days. And it wasn't as if he came across people very much at all.

It wasn't a man at all.

It was a small child. A young girl. About his own daughter's age.

What was she doing out here all alone?

He could see her fairly well. She didn't seem to see him, so he kept his head up for a few more minutes, getting a better look at her.

She carried a handgun.

Her clothes were ratty and worn out. But they were more or less clean. And they weren't as ratty as one might expect them to be.

Based on her appearance, Terry doubted that she was all alone in the world. She must have belonged to some family or group.

Maybe she was lost. Maybe she'd been separated from her group, and she was trying to find them again.

Terry thought he saw her looking in his direction, and he ducked his head back down.

Suddenly, a diabolical thought popped into Terry's head.

Before the EMP, he'd been trying to become a professional helper, someone who helped people. But now? Now he was desperate. Now he needed to do something.

He needed to take action.

The plan hatched in his head, coming to him almost fully formed.

Whoever this girl belonged to; they'd likely do anything to get her back. Or at least give up plenty of their food or supplies. And possibly some information crucial to learning the secret stores and supply areas where they got their goods.

Terry didn't waste any time. He felt invigorated with the possibilities of kidnapping this girl.

He didn't bother to think of the consequences, of the harm he would do. After all, he was, in most ways, a broken man. A shadow of his former self.

Terry popped himself up into the standing position, ignoring the various aches and pains in his body.

He kept his weapons holstered and away. He stuck his two hands up in the air, his palms open, as if he was surrendering.

He walked forward slowly, towards the girl walking alone.

"Don't shoot!" he called out. "I come in peace!"

He knew that she wouldn't shoot him. No matter how battle-hardened she was, she wouldn't shoot a man with his hands in the air. An adult might have. But a kid? No way.

There was a small smirk on Terry's face that he couldn't conceal, no matter what. But he doubted she'd notice it.

He was going to use his cunning rather than his weapons. His mind rather than his guns.

And he knew for sure that he could outsmart a young girl.

Soon enough, he'd be handing her over to her people, and receiving a glorious bounty as payment.

He and his family would be safe.

And he'd be the hero. The man who'd taken action. The man who wasn't afraid, and was never weak.

5

MAX

The lackey gave Max a hard shove, and Max found himself falling face-first onto the stockade's dirt floor.

"That'll teach you," said the lackey, slamming the door closed.

Max heard the click of a lock. And another. The sound of footsteps.

And then he was alone.

His hands were still bound, making it hard to get to his feet.

But he managed. One leg at a time, using his hands together to help himself up.

He wasn't the type of man who stayed down. If there was anything Max was good at it, it was pressing on, and picking himself up.

There'd always be setbacks. There'd always be problems with the plan. If you didn't understand that, Max knew, small problems were liable to completely derail you.

It wasn't as if Max was in the best of spirits, though.

The trick was to not let himself get too down. Not let himself sink into the spiral of doubt and despair.

And to do that, all he needed to do was find the next step. And do it.

He'd been cocky, maybe. He'd gotten himself picked up at that Jeep in the road. He should have hung back farther.

And then he'd made another crucial error, which was demanding too much too soon. After all, he hadn't even tried to prove himself.

No wonder they'd thrown him in the pen.

Maybe that's what he deserved.

Or maybe not.

He didn't know where he was going to end up, but he knew that he wasn't going to stay locked up for long. One way or another, he'd get out.

Max was back on his feet.

Looking around, he surveyed the area.

The stockade was an outdoor area bordered by a tall fence made of wire. The fence was at least twenty-five feet tall. At the top of the fence, there was a thick spiral of barbed wire.

There was a single door to the stockade, made of metal and thick wire. It appeared as if there were various key-only padlocks, as well as a built-in deadbolt.

Max was impressed by the fence and the door. Impressed with the level of infrastructure that this camp had managed to attain in a relatively short time.

Obviously there were people at the camp who understood construction well enough to build this. And they'd had to get the materials too. Not just any materials, because this stockade obviously wasn't just tossed together haphazardly. Instead, it was a building based on a plan and rigorous specifications.

But that didn't mean Max couldn't escape from it if he decided that's what the situation required.

He'd take it all in first. Then decide what to do.

His wrists were hurting from the plastic binders, which were cinched on too tight. But he ignored it.

His stomach was rumbling with hunger. It'd been a long time since he'd eaten.

But he was used to going hungry. Hell, most everyone was at this point.

His leg hurt. It always hurt. He could deal with that. A little pain never killed anyone.

His pack was gone. Confiscated. Same with his Glock and his knives. It was a blow. Hopefully it was temporary.

Outside the fence, there was all manner of activity. There were men pushing wheelbarrows full of supplies that looked like they'd been pilfered from various big box stores.

The men with the wheelbarrows were dressed in decent clothes. Not a lot of rips and tears. They looked fairly well fed, too.

Other men and women were walking here and there. Some carried clipboards that they studied. Others seemed to be surveying everything, standing there with their arms behind their backs, watching.

It seemed to be a well-organized militia. Plenty of work going on. Plenty of food available.

Everyone was armed with at least a handgun. Many had long guns.

Some men wore pieces of police or military uniforms. No one had a complete uniform. Max knew that the clothes didn't mean anything. The men might or might not have been members of the police force or military.

Max turned his attention to the inside of the stockade.

There wasn't much there.

On the other end of it, about a hundred yards away, there were a couple figures curled up, leaning against the fence.

The stockade was made to house a lot of men. That might mean something about what plans the leaders of the militia had. What tricks they had up their sleeves.

Max made his way across the dirt. He moved slowly, not wanting to draw much attention to himself.

Outside the fence, there seemed to be just one guard who paced back and forth. His eyes stayed trained on Max.

To Max's surprise, one of the figures huddled up against the fence was a woman. He only noticed it as he got closer to her. She didn't look up at him, and neither did the man next to her.

Both of them were thinner than everyone else on the other side of the fence. Max supposed that meant they'd been locked up for a while. Or maybe not.

Max nodded vaguely at them, and sat himself down against the fence, next to the woman.

He wanted information. But he didn't want to appear too eager. He needed to play it cool.

Max sat there for about an hour without a single thing happening. He didn't know the exact time because his trusty Vostok watch had been confiscated by the lackey who'd thrown him into the stockade.

It wasn't a good feeling, not having his gear. After all, the gear had gotten him through tough times. It had always been there. Sort of like a friend.

But he knew he'd get it back somehow. And he still had his most important tool of all. His mind.

A watch, a gun, or a knife were only good so far as one knew how to use them. Without a plan, without a mind behind the tools, they were just objects. Objects that looked nice but did nothing.

As Max sat there, he tried not to let his thoughts wander back to his camp, back to Mandy and to his unborn child. He knew that if he let his mind drift too far in that direction, he'd get lost in worries and doubts.

Max tried to remind himself that if he didn't return to Mandy, she and the child would still be taken care of. Max trusted Georgia with his and Mandy's lives. Not to mention his brother. And the others.

And Mandy could take care of herself as well. It wasn't as if she was a weakling. Max had watched her do horrible things to bad people. He'd watched her defend herself in the most dangerous of situations. He'd watched her go on and on and never let herself stop, no matter what.

Max had trusted Mandy with his own life countless times. She was competent. She was intelligent. And strong. And she'd be the mother of his child, whether or not he returned.

Still, Max wanted to live. He wanted to return to Mandy.

He needed to return.

And to do that, he needed to forget, temporarily, about Mandy.

He also couldn't let his attention focus on his disappointment. He'd spent a long time getting to this camp. He'd had high hopes. Hopes of restoring order to the country. Hopes that he himself could play an important role, that he could help start to squash the chaos that had overtaken the land.

Max needed to remember that just because he'd been imprisoned it didn't mean that the militia wasn't good, that Grant wasn't a good man.

Max hadn't yet met Grant or seen any sign of him. And

nothing else about the camp made him think that anything bad was going on.

Max had simply been overzealous, overconfident, and too cocky for his own good. What had he been thinking, demanding a position and audience like that?

If he'd approached the whole thing in a humble way, maybe the outcome would have been completely different.

But Max had that pride deep inside him. It was the pride that he'd earned from surviving countless situations in which he knew he should have died. He'd earned it by going and going, no matter what.

Max kept his attention focused on his immediate surroundings, on the men and women who were at work outside the stockade, and on the guard.

When Max had been thrown in the stockade, no one had read him any rights. No one had told him about due process. No one had told him what would happen to him, or whether he could expect a trial or not.

The militia camp here was its own government. It answered to no one. It was all powerful. It didn't have any obligation to read Max any rights.

So Max didn't know what would happen to him.

From the looks of it, the man and woman next to him against the fence had been in here for quite a while.

The fact that Max and these two other prisoners were alive didn't mean much. Max wanted to believe it meant that the militia wasn't killing people, that instead it was just imprisoning them. Besides, Max was sure that were plenty of other militia groups who would have just shot him, rather than going to the trouble of incarcerating him.

After all, having prisoners meant feeding them, giving them water, possibly treating their medical issues.

Having prisoners was a good sign, in that sense. It meant

a high level of organization. A high level of control over the population of the camp.

But Max knew that for each prisoner in the stockade, there might well have been ten corpses out in a ditch somewhere. Maybe they were planning on killing Max after interrogating him in a couple hours. Or maybe there was some other reason to keep him alive for now. Maybe others had not been so lucky.

Max's mind was strategic. He couldn't help it. He was always analyzing, always coming up with plans.

If it came to escaping, Max doubted he'd be able to go out the way he came in. He'd either need a key or he'd have to pick or break the lock.

While Max understood the fundamentals of lock picking, and had practiced before on a couple, he doubted he'd be able to pull it off in this situation. Max knew that realistically appraising his own abilities was important. Without the proper tools and plenty of time, he likely wouldn't be able to pick the lock.

Getting the key itself was an option. Most likely, the guard had it.

But the guard was armed. And he wouldn't want to just hand over the key.

Attacking the guard was a possibility. After all, Max might be able to reach through the fencing to strangle the guard or incapacitate him in some other way. Then he could remove the key and open the gate.

But attacking the guard was a long shot. It sounded more like something that might work on a television show than in real life. After all, the guard would surely fight back.

Max figured that his best chance was also the simplest. His idea was to just wait until no one was looking and then climb over the fence.

Sure, there was barbed wire at the top. And it would cut him up to hell. And he'd bleed plenty, the blood trickling back down the fence. But he could deal with it. He'd dealt with worse. If he was really lucky, he could find something to blunt the barbed wire with a little. Throw a blanket over it or something.

Not that there were any blankets around. The best he'd be able to manage would be some article of clothing.

It was likely that the guards had already thought about people climbing over the fence. Unless they didn't mind people escaping. Surely, they'd have something in place to prevent it. After all, barbed wire was extremely inconvenient and painful, but it didn't stop everyone. Especially not the most determined people.

Maybe there was another guard out of sight, waiting to shoot anyone at the top of the fence.

Or maybe there was something else. Something Max couldn't think of at the moment.

So maybe that wasn't the best plan after all. It was too easy. And the militia seemed too organized to overlook something so obvious. So tempting.

Max frowned slightly as his mind kept churning, looking for another plan.

He didn't come up with much. Except that he'd wait and see how the food was delivered. If someone came in through that gate, maybe there'd be an opportunity there somewhere.

Max's gaze shifted away from the men laboring with the wheelbarrows to the fencing itself.

If only he had some wire cutters, he could cut right through that fencing.

Then he thought of it.

Digging.

He could dig under the fence.

The dirt was loose. A little damp. Perfect for digging at with his hands.

Sure, he wouldn't be able to dig very far. But he didn't need to.

He just needed to dig a little shallow patch beneath the fencing. The way a dog would. He was thin enough that he could squeeze himself under it, provided that he could bend the fencing a little.

But surely, the militia guard would have thought of this possibility too.

Max was getting exhausted, thinking through all the possibilities.

And he didn't yet even know if he needed to escape or not.

Would it be better to wait and see what happened? Wait to see whether they would give him a second chance, some kind of audience.

No, probably not. It seemed just as likely they'd kill him.

Max didn't want to take any chances.

He wanted to live. He wanted to survive. It was just a drive he had. An intense one, like some little motor that kept on chugging and chugging, deep in his body, no matter what happened.

There was no point in thinking about his crushed dreams of restored order.

He just needed to live.

He could think about it all later.

Suddenly, after over an hour of silence, the woman next to him stirred. She shifted her position, and in doing so, turned to face Max.

For the first time, Max saw her face.

She was a young woman. Early twenties, probably.

But she looked old. Ancient, even.

Her face looked haggard. Lines everywhere. Gaunt, as if all the fat had been stripped from her body. And not in a good way. More like an unhealthy, starvation kind of way.

She looked old beyond her years.

But her eyes were still young. That's how he knew her real age.

There was pain in her expression.

She spoke with care, as if the words themselves caused her pain.

"They'll keep us in here until we die," she said.

"Why?" said Max. "What do they have to gain?"

"They take us," she said. "And they do experiments on us."

A chill ran up Max's spine.

"Experiments?" he said. "What kind of experiments?"

The woman didn't answer. She just stared at him.

It was a horrible stare. There was something in those young eyes of hers that said something. Something that couldn't be put into words.

The chill didn't leave Max's spine. And he knew that he wasn't going to wait around to see what happened. He was going to try to escape. Tonight, if at all possible.

"And don't think about escaping," she said, her hoarse voice continuing, almost as a coda to Max's thoughts. "They're harder on you when you try to escape."

That wasn't good to hear.

But Max wasn't going to give up easily either.

He'd gotten himself into all this. Walked right into a trap. Fallen for tales of a charismatic leader. Marched right on in. Foolish.

Well, he wasn't going to stay anyone's fool.

6

SADIE

Sadie had been walking through the woods next to the road. She didn't want to walk on the road since it would increase her chances of running into someone. Even though she was feeling rebellious, she didn't want to throw caution to the wind.

Which is why she walked with her handgun at the ready. Finger right on the trigger guard.

Suddenly, up ahead, a man popped up.

Had he been lying in wait? Lying in hiding?

He stuck both of his hands into the air immediately.

Sadie's finger went to the trigger.

He was a little too far away for a clean shot, judging by what she'd learned from her mother during target practice.

But she might be able to make it.

She got ready to shoot. Legs apart. Arms outstretched. Both hands on the gun.

Slow, steady breaths. Her adrenaline was already spiking. She didn't want to let it interfere if she had to shoot.

As far as she could tell, the man's hands were empty. He

turned them now, making a point of showing her his empty palms.

He was a thin man. He had the look of someone who had lost a lot of weight in a short time. Not too healthy looking.

"Don't shoot!" he called out.

His voice was a little hoarse.

He didn't sound like a bad guy. Nothing bad in his voice. But Sadie, even though she was young, had been through enough to know that it didn't mean anything. Appearances could be deceiving.

Sadie was keenly aware that she might be walking into a trap. Her eyes didn't leave the man for long, but they did dart around, looking to see if there were signs of anyone else present.

If there were someone else, they could easily be hidden. Behind a log. Behind a tree. Simply lying on the ground might make them invisible to Sadie. And, as she knew well from her mother, a man with a rifle and a scope could be quite far away and still in range.

But if that were the case, what was the point of setting up a trap like this? It wouldn't have made sense.

If there were a rifleman that wanted to shoot her, he could have just shot her from a distance, without all the complications of having a man standing there with his hands in the air.

So it probably wasn't that kind of trap.

But it still could have been a trap.

"Why aren't you speaking?" shouted Sadie, her voice rising a little. She was keenly aware that her voice was that of a child, rather than an adult. "What do you want?"

"Nothing," said the man, his voice cracking a little. He

sounded hoarse, as if he hadn't spoken in a long time, or as if he'd gone through some kind of extreme stress.

Sadie was stumped. She was silent. Thinking.

"I'm not going to hurt you," shouted the man.

"That doesn't mean anything," said Sadie.

She took a few slow steps forward. Her idea was to get closer to the man. Better chance at a good shot, if she had to shoot him. And a better chance of seeing if he was up to something.

"Look," said the man. "I'm just trying to get home to my family. I don't want any trouble."

"Why did you immediately surrender?" called out Sadie. She was still walking forward. She could see the man's face more clearly. He looked weary and thin. Not to mention unhealthy. Especially compared to Max and John and the other adults at her camp. "And why didn't you just stay hidden?"

The whole situation was weird to Sadie. She'd been involved in countless confrontations with strangers. But none of them had gone like this. It seemed that no one in their right mind would immediately surrender. And especially not to a child.

She was keenly aware that she was still a child. Even at a distance, the man towered above her. As she aimed her gun, she had to hold her arms up at an angle, so that she was aiming up, rather than straight across, as an adult would.

"I don't know," said the man. "I'm too tired and weak. I'm just..." His words trailed off into nothing.

"You're what?"

"I'm just trying to get back to my family," he said. It sounded as if he was on the verge of tears, almost choking on his words.

"Why don't you answer the question?"

"I didn't think I was strong enough to fight. You would have come across me eventually. I'm weak. I've been giving all my food to my family. I thought I'd find something on this trip, but I didn't..."

Sadie was close enough to the man to really study his face. He did look weak and weary.

Maybe he was telling the truth.

And maybe he wasn't.

Sadie didn't know what to do. If Max were there, he would have known what to do. And her mother would have too.

Sadie tried to think back to other situations. How would Max or her mother have handled them?

Well, she couldn't remember them coming across a situation quite like this.

"Who are you with?" said the man.

"Who am I with?"

"Yeah. You're obviously from around here. Living around here, I mean. With a group. There's no way you're on your own. For one thing, you don't have enough gear with you for a long journey."

"I'm not telling you shit," said Sadie. "Answer the questions yourself."

"OK," said the man. "Like I said, I have a family. A wife and a daughter. We live not far from here. A little house. A regular house. But it's kind of out of the way. We've had a lot of trouble. But we've managed to survive somehow. Just barely."

"You have a daughter?" said Sadie, her ears perking up at the mention of it.

Was it possible that this was the family she was looking for? The family with the daughter about her age?

Maybe she didn't need to fear this man after all.

"Yeah. And you know what? She's about your age."

What were the chances that this was really the family she was looking for? They seemed to be getting greater.

Sadie didn't want to give away too much information about herself. But she wanted to confirm the story somehow.

"There was a guy who came by our camp a while ago," said Sadie. "And he told us about a family that lived nearby... He said that there was a little girl about my age. He must have spent some time with you, if you're from the same family. Do you know his name?"

There was a smile on the man's face. "It was a weird name," he said. "He went by Holstead."

Sadie felt relief pouring through her body.

She let her arms lower, the muzzle of her gun pointing now harmlessly at the ground.

Sadie was walking towards him. She didn't feel scared anymore. And not only that, she felt relief.

She'd accidentally stumbled on the girl's father. How lucky was that?

"So your daughter's about my age?" said Sadie.

The man nodded. "I'd guess so," said the man. "I bet you don't get to play with a lot of girls your age, right?"

Sadie shook her head. "Not since the EMP."

"My daughter's always saying the same thing," he said. "She misses her friends. It's been really hard for her, not having anyone but her parents around. I'm afraid we're just not always great company. And there are always all these problems. All these things that we have to deal with."

Sadie nodded vigorously. The smile on her face was growing by the minute. "I don't even know what happened to my friends," she said. "And my brother, well, he's a little bit older, but he doesn't want to play any games with me."

"And I bet talking to him isn't the same as talking to your friends back at school, right?"

"Not at all," said Sadie. She was feeling understood. Really understood. For the first time in a while.

She was getting really close to the man.

He still had his hands in the air. Almost as if he'd forgotten all about them.

Sadie studied his face again, now that she was closer.

He did look worn out. Weary.

There was a smile on his face. Almost a grin, really.

The smile made him seem even more trustworthy.

It seemed like he was a good guy after all. A dad. A dad who smiled when thinking about his daughter.

He was just a good guy on hard times. That's what had put the marks of weariness and weakness on his face.

"Do you want to meet her, my daughter, I mean?" said the man.

Sadie was just about two feet from him now. "Of course," she said, not knowing if she should mention that she'd been looking for this man's daughter.

No, better not mention it. It sounded too improbable. Too strange.

She wanted to seem normal. As if this was just a happy accident.

And it was, really.

"Great," said the man. "I'm Terry, by the way."

"Nice to meet you. I'm Sadie."

Terry nodded.

Sadie suddenly started giggling.

"What is it?"

"You can put your hands down," she said, a smirk on her

face. It seemed really funny that he still had his hands in the air. Maybe the funniest thing she'd seen in a long time. Maybe the only funny thing she'd seen, come to think of it.

After all, in a normal situation, before the EMP, she would have shaken the hand of a friend's father. Not pointed a gun at him, his hands up in the air.

And it also seemed funny that an adult man would surrender immediately to a child.

A child with a gun, though.

Terry finally put his hands down and grinned sheepishly. "That's funny," he said. "Really funny."

And he started to laugh.

His mouth hung open as he laughed.

It was a big laugh. One that seemed to echo.

It was a little strange, and Sadie looked up at him, waiting for him to stop.

Finally, he did, after what seemed like a long time.

"Well," he said. "Come on. Let's go. My daughter will be really excited to meet you."

Sadie grinned. She was excited. This, after all, was what she'd been after.

"The only thing is, though," said Terry, "won't your parents wonder where you've gone?"

"Not for a little while," said Sadie. "My mom's asleep. She won't wake up until the afternoon. She had a night shift."

"Ah," said Terry. There was a look on his face as if he was considering something carefully. "Why don't you tell me more about your mom, and the others, while we walk?"

"OK," said Sadie, eagerly.

It was nice to talk to someone new. Someone she hadn't talked to before. Someone who was eager and interested in her life. Someone who seemed to understand her.

She and Terry set off, walking side by side, towards

Terry's home, the home that he shared with his wife and daughter.

Georgia had fallen asleep in the back of a pickup truck, with a sleeping bag draped over her.

Normally she slept in a lean-to structure. But sometimes lately she'd been wanting to sleep outdoors more. Not that the lean-to really felt like "indoors."

She didn't know why she'd felt like this, like she always wanted to be outside, no matter what. Maybe it had something to do with a feeling she'd been experiencing over the last few months.

It was the feeling of being trapped. Of not having any options. Of having to stay in the same place all the time.

Georgia had never been the type of woman to be content staying at home, cooking and doing the housework. That's why she'd always had to take those hunting trips. That's why she'd often had a gig of driving around, delivering one thing or another, either as a main job or just a side gig.

She'd always liked the feeling of being on the move. Of being out and about.

And since the EMP, she'd been constantly on the move.

She'd often wished they'd had a safe haven, rather than running from one spot to the next.

And now that they had their safe haven? Now that the hordes had been killed off? Well, she was happy for the safety. For the security.

But she couldn't shake the feeling that they were stuck. That they were sitting ducks. That sooner or later something would come along and get them.

When she slept in the night, she'd bolt awake at least once an hour, drenched in sweat, her heart pounding, reaching for her gun.

The first thing she thought of was: who's there? What's the threat?

The second thing she always thought of was: where are Sadie and James? Are they safe?

Waking up after a full night's sleep was a little different. She'd managed to calm herself down each time she'd woken up in a cold sweat. By the time she woke up after about seven hours of sleep, she was tired, rather than well rested. But at least she was no longer sweating.

Georgia pushed the sleeping bag off her. It was still damp from the sweat from earlier that "night."

The night, of course, had really been the daytime.

She was exhausted as she hauled herself out of the truck bed. Her muscles ached. Her joints ached. It seemed like her bones even ached, although she didn't know if that was even possible.

Night was starting to settle. Dusk was falling.

Had she slept longer than she'd meant to?

There was movement around the camp. People coming and going from the various structures.

She glanced at her wrist, expecting to see the time on a watch.

Almost to her surprise, there was a watch, one that Max had found for her a week ago on a dead man's wrist. (The man had apparently starved to death, out on the nearby highway, wasting away to almost literal skin and bone.) She'd gotten used to not having a watch that worked. She'd trashed her own watch right after the EMP, still keeping the habit of looking at her wrist.

Most watches from the pre-EMP world were quartz watches, which meant that they kept time by way of a vibrating quartz crystal. They were commonly known as "digital" watches, but even watches with an analog face were usually powered by quartz crystals.

It turned out that all the quartz watches had been destroyed from the EMP. Or at least all the quartz watches that they'd managed to find so far. Max had said that he'd expected to find some that had been shielded, either by their accidental placement somewhere, or intentionally, by their own case design.

But so far mechanical watches were the only time-keeping devices that seemed to still work. Georgia remembered seeing the inside of one when she was a kid. It had been her father's watch, which had become too inaccurate, and he was cursing at it as he tried to adjust it himself. All he'd ended up doing was mangling the miniature gears inside of it, and it had never worked properly again.

Unfortunately, most mechanical watches, unless they were expensive, were not that accurate. The few that Max and the others had come across on dead men and women (mostly men) didn't keep very good time.

It seemed that the one Georgia wore now had gone from keeping time very badly (at least a few minutes slow each day) to not working at all. The watch had stopped right at three o'clock, all three hands frozen.

She shook her wrist, thinking that the power reserve of the watch was weak, and that it needed to be moved around a little, to start it back up.

Unfortunately, nothing happened. The second hand remained motionless no matter how much she shook it.

Annoyed, Georgia took off the watch and tossed it aside, not caring where it fell.

It was just a piece of junk. Worthless.

Then she realized that someone might be able to get it working again. After all, John seemed to possess some strange knack for getting things going again, when no one else could. It was strange, because Max and Georgia were both much more mechanically minded than John was.

Better save the watch. It was a lesson they'd all had to learn at one point or another. Throw nothing away. Who knew when you'd get anything like it ever again?

She had to hunt for it, getting annoyed with herself for discarding it.

It was a huge, garish watch. Not to her taste at all. Neon colors all around it. Strange shapes for the hands. An astoundingly cluttered dial. Simply distasteful in all respects.

It had looked ridiculous on her wrist.

She'd hoped that it'd be at least easier to find among the dead leaves and weeds, due to its large size.

Georgia was getting madder by the minute now.

Where was that watch?

Her stomach was rumbling, and she remembered that she hadn't eaten any dinner.

She'd been too exhausted at the end of her watch shift and had just hit the sack right away.

Suddenly, a cry of pain pierced the air. A female sound.

Higher pitched than a sound a man would make. Probably, at least. No way to know for sure.

Georgia's heart started to beat rapidly. Her head snapped around, towards the direction of the sound.

Her hand went to her handgun. Fingers wrapped around the grip. Flicked the safety off.

Sometimes, safety meant shooting the enemy dead as quickly as possible.

Her legs were already moving, and she sprinted her way towards the other end of camp, weaving through the scattered trees.

A noise to her right. Heavy footsteps. Panting.

Georgia's head turned. Eyes shifting to the right, her gun reflexively followed her eyes.

"Georgia! It's me!"

It was John. Running alongside her. Running for the same reason she was. Headed towards the source of the noise.

Georgia didn't answer. Her gun went away from him.

They kept running.

"I think it's Mandy," John managed to say, breathless.

Georgia's mind went right to the baby.

She could tell that John was already thinking along those lines.

Out of nowhere, Cynthia appeared. "Was it Mandy?" she said.

They'd almost reached her.

Max and Mandy shared a little hut that could almost be called cute. They'd worked hard on it together.

Now Mandy lived there alone, waiting for Max to return, getting ready for the birth of their baby.

Of course, no one had any idea what the sex of the baby

would be. Those days were gone. And, more disconcertingly, no one knew if the baby would be healthy.

All they'd been able to do was to make sure that Mandy got as much food as she wanted. And that she got a good variety of food. That way she hopefully got the vitamins, minerals, not to mention calories that were so crucial for the development of another human.

Georgia could see the little hut up ahead. Mandy was nowhere to be seen. But her voice had definitely come from this direction. She was inside. That was the most likely scenario.

As Mandy had gotten farther along in her pregnancy, Georgia and the others had requested that she stop doing her normal duties. They'd wanted her to stop doing her watch shift, gathering firewood, and going on expeditions.

Mandy had been a tough sell, to say the least. It had been almost impossible to get her to give up even the watch shifts. And no one really liked taking a shift. Especially not the ones in the middle of the night.

But Mandy was tough. And she wanted to remain useful for as long as possible during the pregnancy. The way she told it; she was only trying to help the group. And helping the group was really selfish, because it wasn't like her kid was going to live very long without the support of everyone else.

Another scream came. Definitely Mandy's. And it definitely came from the little hut ahead.

Georgia's long legs gave her a good advantage when running. She may have been older than John, but not by much. And she could still outrun him. Especially now that she'd recovered so well from her injuries.

She pulled ahead of John and reached the hut first.

There wasn't really a door, so much as a blanket that had been hung up like a curtain.

Georgia didn't bother to knock as she normally would. She just dove right in, crouching down so that she didn't knock her head on the ceiling or the doorframe.

"Mandy!" she cried out.

There was no one else inside the hut.

Just Mandy.

Just Mandy with her back against the wall, sitting. Her knees were pulled up around her large belly.

There was an expression of pain on her face. Intense pain. Her mouth was puckered. It looked like she was breathing heavy.

Georgia tucked her gun away. There was no need for that which was good. She was glad someone wasn't there, threatening pregnant Mandy.

But Mandy had screamed. Now that the other option was eliminated, what else was there?

Evidently the pregnancy itself. And it'd be an early one, if that were the case. Which meant that, without a hospital, the baby wasn't likely to survive.

The other option was that it was some other complication of pregnancy.

It wasn't a subject that Georgia knew much about. Or anything about at all. For her own pregnancies, she'd gone to the hospital, just like every other woman she'd known. There hadn't been any complications, but the doctors and nurses had been there around the clock. They'd given her an epidural, and they'd been there to soothe her and tell her that everything was OK.

Georgia didn't feel like she could do the same for Mandy. Because, here in the woods, there weren't any machines or devices that would tell Georgia that everything was OK.

Georgia put her arms on Mandy's shoulders.

"What is it, Mandy?"

John entered a moment later, ducking down. Cynthia followed him.

Both had their guns drawn, and both holstered them upon evaluating the situation.

"We thought you'd been attacked," said John.

"You're not going into labor, are you?" said Cynthia.

"Something's wrong," said Mandy. "Something's not right..."

"Tell me what you're feeling," said Georgia.

Mentally, Georgia was anything but calm, but she made sure to keep her voice as calm as she possibly could.

If there was anything she'd learned from her own pregnancies, with James and Sadie, it was that having someone freaking out next to you did *not* help.

For a second, she had a flashback to her ex-husband. He'd been there for James's birth, but not Sadie's. By that point, he'd been long gone. A total loser. And she'd known it all along. She should have just left him from the beginning.

But, then again, she would not have been blessed with James and Sadie. She may have had a tougher exterior than just about anyone else, but inside, she could be a softie. At least when it came to her children.

If anything ever happened to them, she knew that she'd hurt too much. She knew that she'd have to bury the pain, and the only way she'd be able to do that would be with violence. Extreme violence directed at whoever was responsible.

Her ex-husband's dumb obnoxious face seemed to hang in her mind's eye for a moment.

Then she shook it off.

"I'm feeling weak," said Mandy. "Really weak. Like I couldn't stand up anymore."

"You couldn't stand up?" said John, his voice rising. His distress and worry were plainly evident in his tone.

Cynthia tugged on his arm, giving him a look to tell him to shut up. Georgia supposed that as a woman Cynthia understood more what pregnancy meant.

It was strange, she suddenly realized that she'd never talked to Cynthia about whether or not she'd had children. For all she knew, Cynthia did have kids, and understood well the process of childbirth.

If she did have kids, it seemed more polite not to ask about them. After all, who knew what could have happened to them. Georgia did remember that Cynthia had had a husband who'd died right after the EMP. But she'd only heard it secondhand from John one night.

"I'll take care of this," said Georgia, turning to address John. "Why don't you wait outside. We'll let you know if we need you. Plus, the others might want to know what happened, if they heard the screaming."

Mandy suddenly let out another scream. Georgia saw the pain on her face. It was definitely real.

Cynthia muttered something under her breath.

There were beads of sweat on Mandy's brow. Some of her hair had come loose from the bun she'd had it in, and it was plastered wet against her forehead.

John gave a nod and disappeared out the door.

The space was small, and fairly cluttered with odds and ends, things that Max had been tinkering with. Knives he'd been trying to get a good edge on again, or broken compasses he'd been trying to reassemble. Maps he'd been drawing routes on, or just studying.

"Take her pulse, would you?" said Georgia, noticing that Cynthia had on a watch. She hoped that hers worked.

Cynthia moved to Mandy's side, taking her hand and putting her fingers on her wrist, while watching the dial on her watch.

"Now tell me where it hurts, Mandy," said Georgia, taking Mandy's other hand. It was her attempt at a comforting gesture. Not necessarily her strong suit.

Mandy said nothing. Instead, she pointed at her belly.

Cynthia looked over at Georgia, and they exchanged a look.

The meaning of the look was clear.

Neither of them knew what was going on.

But they both knew that it wasn't good.

For some reason, Wilson couldn't get that man from earlier that day out of his head.

Wilson had sent many men and women to the stockades before. He'd sent many to be executed. He thought that he'd gotten used to it all.

After all, what did it matter if a few people were sacrificed, so long as there was a good cause? As long as they were doing important work, a few lives here and there were all part of the deal. Part of what had to happen.

How many lives had been lost overall since the EMP? Hundreds of thousands? Millions?

Whatever the number, it was a lot.

Of course, somewhere in Wilson's files were the official estimates on the death toll. Not to mention the death toll in the coming months.

They weren't going to restore order to the nation without some good solid numbers.

And without a fair bit of paperwork as well.

It was getting late. Wilson was tired, and his back was

aching. Maybe he should put in an order for a better chair. He did deserve it, after all, as Grant was always telling him.

Wilson put out the candle that was still burning on his desk and slowly stood up, grabbing his lower back with both hands and letting out a groan of pain.

"Anyone there?" came a gruff, familiar voice from outside the tent.

It was Grant. His voice was unmistakable.

Wilson felt his heart start to beat a little faster. Even after all the time he'd spent with Grant, Grant's presence still made him a little nervous. Not that he'd ever admit that. Maybe not even to himself.

"Hey, Grant," said Wilson.

The tent flap moved back, and Grant stepped into the room.

He had a commanding presence. He was taller than most men. And well built. A good amount of muscle. But he didn't seem like the type who spent a lot of time working out. More likely, it had just come naturally to him.

He was probably a little thinner than he had been before the EMP. But weren't they all?

After all, they were on strict rations here at the camp. Everyone was. Even Grant. And those in charge of the mess halls were strict. Very strict. Men had been sent to the stockade for a week just for trying to plunder a few hundred extra calories.

It suddenly occurred to Wilson that he didn't have any idea what Grant had done before the EMP. Which was strange. It was almost as if Grant were made for a post-apocalyptic world. It seemed as if he had just shown up, his ideas and mindset already fully formed, ready to lead. And people had been ready to follow.

Grant stood there, arms crossed, surveying the tent. "You really must like paperwork, you bastard."

"Someone's got to do it, and I've got a talent for it, apparently."

"That you do, my friend, that you do."

They spoke sometimes in a casual way, as if they were friends. And in some ways they were, but there was always a distance around Grant. Wilson was the closest to him, and he felt far away.

Grant said nothing more, and a long silence hung in the tent. The silence made Wilson feel nervous. Anxious.

It was strange. Wilson felt almost as if he were in trouble for something. That was the way Grant made him feel sometimes. But Wilson knew he'd done an excellent job on everything. Hell, he was practically running the camp, while Grant did whatever it was that Grant did all day.

"What's on your mind, Grant?" said Wilson, breaking the silence. His voice cracked a little as he spoke, due to his nerves, as if he were a teenager.

"I thought we'd go for a little walk," said Grant. "Just the two of us. A nighttime stroll."

Grant said nothing more. Offered no explanation.

"All right," said Wilson. He knew it wasn't a good idea to contradict Wilson. He'd seen men do it before.

The last thing Wilson wanted to do right now was tell Grant that he didn't feel like going for a walk.

And the truth was that he didn't feel like it. After all, it was late. His back hurt. And he was tired. And he didn't see the point in puttering around in the darkness. That was the duty of those who had night-watch shifts, and those who had other responsibilities.

Wilson followed Grant out of the tent.

The night was upon them. There was darkness every-where, punctuated by the odd lantern, candle, or flashlight.

Flashlights were in short supply, despite the abundance of supplies that the militia had managed to secure through countless raids and expeditions.

Wilson knew that Grant had a couple of his own flash-lights. After all, as a leader, he was entitled to the best gear.

But Grant didn't pull one out. Instead, he just stepped out into the darkness and started walking at a brisk pace. His long legs moved rapidly.

Wilson had to practically jog to keep up. He tried to stay abreast of Grant, but it was difficult, and he kept finding himself lagging behind.

The activity of the camp had certainly died down since the daytime, but there was still quite a bit going on. After all, things had to get done. Wilson had signed off on a lot of the orders himself. So there were plenty of men and women who were going to work all the through the night tonight. They'd sleep during the day, of course.

Their camp was huge. At least a 1,000 men and women. Wilson couldn't remember the exact population figure at the moment.

The camp spread for miles. And it seemed as if Grant wanted to walk to the camp's edge tonight, because he never stopped. He just wound his way through the lines of men and women working away, with Wilson trotting behind him.

They'd walked in silence for half an hour, when Wilson had almost had enough of it all. After all, he was huffing and puffing. His legs ached and his stomach rumbled with hunger. He'd skipped his dinner that night, and had been planning on having it right before bed. But now, it seemed that there was no dinner in sight.

Wilson was really lagging behind now. He could just see Grant's back. And the back of his head.

Grant wasn't slowing down at all. And he never once turned around to see if Wilson was still there.

"What's this all about anyway, Grant?" said Wilson, in a rare moment of sticking up for himself. "I was thinking I'd be hitting the sack around now."

Grant stopped dead in his tracks. Turned around.

Wilson almost ran smack into him. But he stopped too.

Grant stared right at him.

They were near a man who appeared to be digging a trench. The man wore a headlamp, and its very pale white light cast strange stark shadows on Grant's face. There in the shadows, there in the darkness, he had never looked more severe or imposing.

The man who was digging didn't even look up. He looked like he was digging with all the fervor and strength he had, as if he was carrying out severe sentencing, as if he'd be sentenced to death if he stopped. And, for all Wilson knew, that was actually the case. Wilson had a good memory, but he didn't have every penal sentence on the tip of his tongue. There was a reason he used all those clipboards.

"This is about the future," said Grant, his voice low and deep. "This is about strength. This is about doing what's right. This is about..."

Wilson had heard this kind of stuff before. These were the kinds of words that Grant used so successfully to speak to the crowds. They ate this kind of stuff up.

For some reason, Wilson felt that he could speak up about it. Maybe it was because he was tired. Maybe he was just feeling a little impatient for whatever reason.

"Come on, Grant," said Wilson, interrupt him. "I've heard

this all before. It's good stuff, but save it for the crowds, won't you? Just spit it out. What'd you drag me out here in the dark for?"

"I wanted to show you something," said Grant.

"Yeah, yeah," said Wilson.

"Well, if you're that impatient, I can tell you it's only a minute away."

"A minute away?" said Wilson, not bothering to hide the skepticism in his voice. "What's a minute away from here?"

"The stockade," said Grant simply. He turned around and began marching off, his large frame almost disappearing into the darkness.

The man digging the trench suddenly looked up. His headlamp shone directly onto Wilson, who shielded his eyes from the bright light.

What did Grant want to show Wilson at the stockade?

His curiosity piqued, and still just as annoyed as before, Wilson started off. He picked up his pace, trying not to let Grant get out of view.

Grant was either wrong or lying. It took about ten more minutes of rapid walking to reach the stockade.

When they got there, Grant stood there, staring at the fence, with his hands on his hips. His legs were spread more than shoulder-width apart, but he still looked as tall and as imposing as ever.

Wilson was panting, and he doubled over, his hands on his knees, as he gasped for breath.

"Everything all right, sir?" said a guard, approaching Grant somewhat timidly.

Having Grant show up at the stockade, or anywhere for that matter, was unusual. And it was often an anxiety-provoking event for whoever was on duty. Wilson had no doubt that this guard would be telling everyone he knew that Grant himself had shown up on his overnight shift.

Grant didn't answer, he just gave the guard a stiff nod. "How's he doing?"

"Sorry, sir? Who?"

"The new one. The one who came in today."

Grant pointed into the dimness of the stockade. The darkness hid most everything, but there were three figures there, huddled against the fencing.

Wilson couldn't tell that new prisoner, Max, from the others. Not in the darkness.

So how could Grant?

And how did Grant know about the new prisoners? How had he even heard about Max, about some nobody impudent upstart?

"He's... fine, I guess..." said the guard, not really knowing what to say.

"He's not going to be fine pretty soon," growled Grant, his tone of voice changing from its normal low and rumbly tones to downright sinister and vicious.

"Sir?" said the guard.

"Bring him here," growled Grant. "I'm going to personally make sure that this... person... understands the power of my authority."

"This is why you brought me here? So you can torture some nobody prisoner? How do you even know about this?"

"I have ears all over. And I wouldn't exactly call it torture."

Wilson should have remembered the spies. After all, Grant confided in no one, but plenty confided in him. Told him everything.

Wilson didn't know what to make of all this. After all, it wasn't like there were any laws on the books about torture.

Shit, they tortured people all the time at the militia camp. After all, if nothing else, it got the job done. And they typically didn't have time to waste at the camp. If information was needed, it was needed sooner rather than later.

But the real question was why was Grant bothering to do any of this himself?

And why did he want Wilson to see it?

It didn't make sense.

Suddenly, a dull thud. A grunt of pain.

Wilson looked up into the darkness to see the guard roughly dragging the man who had been in his tent only earlier today.

It was the same man. But he was bound and gagged. He didn't struggle as he was dumped roughly at Grant's feet, and he barely reacted as the guard kicked him hard in the stomach.

"That's enough," growled Grant. "I'll take him from here."

9

Terry still couldn't believe his luck. It was almost as if the stars had all aligned to give him just exactly what he'd wanted.

It hadn't been that long after he'd come up with his plan that this girl had delivered herself right to him.

She hadn't been the least bit suspicious. Not after the initial meeting. She'd marched right alongside him all the way to his house.

It was almost sad, hearing her talk for so long about all the kinds of games she wanted to play with his daughter.

Oh, he listened. He lent her a good ear. And he even chimed in with stories of his daughter. Real stories. Telling this girl Sadie all about the types of games she liked to play, and all the fun they'd have together.

Now, Terry was a quick thinker. But not as quick as he would have liked. After all, he did have to come up with his plan more or less on the spot.

He'd never kidnapped anyone before, so he carefully ran through the plan in his head as this girl, Sadie, jabbered on happily about all kinds of things.

It was nice that Sadie was also happy, now that she seemed to trust him so much, to tell him all about the camp where she lived.

Now, Terry knew all about Georgia, Sadie's mother. About Max. About John, and Cynthia, everyone else.

He knew about it all.

And he was boiling inside when he heard about it all. He didn't let on to Sadie. Not in the least bit. But he knew that her mother and the other adults were the people who were responsible for stealing all the supplies in the area. They were the ones who were completely responsible for the downfall of Terry and his family. They were the ones who had kept Terry on a starvation-level diet.

And meanwhile, while the girl talked, Terry concocted his plan.

One option was to bring Sadie into the house with his wife and daughter, with Olivia and Lilly. There'd really be no need to actually "kidnap" her in the traditional sense. He could just let her play with Lilly. Then when Sadie wanted to go home, he could make up some lie about why she couldn't return.

That probably wasn't the best idea. Sooner or later, Sadie would insist on returning home. And then what? He'd have to tie her up? In front of his daughter?

He didn't want to expose Lilly to that kind of stuff. Not if he could help it.

And Terry doubted that his wife would approve. She had always been a gentle soul. Much like himself.

But now he was willing to do what it took. He'd do anything to keep his family alive.

He'd stoop to new lows. It was fine. He was OK with the morality of it.

But he didn't want his wife to see him like that. Doing

these things.

Better to keep Sadie somewhere else. He'd make sure she couldn't get away.

He'd keep her alive. Visit her once a day. Give her food and water. Treat her like a pet or a plant.

It'd work out. It had to.

Surely Sadie's mother cared too much about her to lose her. Surely she'd do anything to get her daughter back. Surely Sadie's mother would be willing to pay any price.

And if Sadie's mother was anything like Terry's wife, she wouldn't think to stoop to violence. Terry would be safe from the mother's wrath, because that's just now how modern mothers were.

Stories of mothers doing anything for their children were from older times. Modern mothers were different. More willing to weep in quiet than to take action. At least's that's how Terry's mother had been. And how Terry's wife currently was.

"And then Max told the guy to get lost," Sadie was saying. Terry hadn't been listening. "The guy didn't want to do it, but he took one look at Max and realized he didn't want to mess with him." Sadie cackled gleefully. She clearly thought a lot of this Max.

"Sounds like he's pretty fearsome," said Terry, speaking almost automatically, as he strategized trying to think of his next move.

"Oh, he is," said Sadie.

Mentally, Terry rolled his eyes.

He doubted Max was really that fearsome. Or scary at all. As far as Terry was concerned, Max was just a thief who was stealing the food that belonged to everyone, namely Terry and his family.

Terry was sure that Sadie's impression of Max was just a

child dreaming that their adult hero was much more capable than he was in reality.

Terry wasn't scared of Max. Or Sadie's mother. Or any of the other thieves. He could handle them.

And after all, no one even knew where Terry lived. Or where he'd taken Sadie.

"Are you OK, Terry?" said Sadie.

"Huh? Yeah. Why?"

"You seem a little distant."

"My stomach hurts," lied Terry.

It was a childish lie. A childish lie for a child.

"It does?" said Sadie.

"Yeah," said Terry.

His mind was racing. Where was he going to take Sadie? It had to be somewhere that was close to his house. Close enough that he could visit. But not far enough away that it took too long. Not far enough that he couldn't keep an eye on her.

And how was he going to get the word out to Sadie's mother? It wasn't like he could send a text message.

A letter, he guessed. He'd have to send a letter.

"It doesn't seem like your stomach hurts."

"Uh-huh," muttered Terry.

"You're being weird," said Sadie.

Terry just nodded, not really listening.

How was he going to keep Sadie captive, anyway? He wished he'd have more time for this plan. Underfed and starving, it didn't seem like his mind was working as well as it should have.

He didn't have chains, did he?

Rope? He couldn't remember.

But there must have been some around the house. Maybe his wife would know.

But then how would he keep Sadie in one place, without exposing her to his wife first?

"Are we almost there?" said Sadie.

It was the classic kid question. His own daughter had asked it relentlessly on car trips. Before the EMP, of course. Now, there was nowhere to go, and no way to get there.

"We're almost there, yeah," said Terry.

"How much longer?"

Terry seemed to wake up. He took stock of his surroundings and realized all of a sudden that they were very close to his home.

"Just a couple more minutes."

"Really?"

"Yeah."

They were crossing an empty street, about to head down a row of small abandoned suburban homes.

They'd never been fancy homes before the EMP. They were the homes of regular people. Blue-collar workers. Honest folks, who'd cared for their property, but hadn't had the money or desire to make their home look like it was something out of a catalog. Instead, things had been kept practical and useful.

Now, the homes had been mostly destroyed.

Terry didn't know who had done it. But he knew when it had happened. Only a couple months ago. After the masses of people from the cities had died off. And a long time after the EMP itself.

The damage done to the homes was senseless. Pointless.

Windows were smashed in. Shuttered ripped off.

People had climbed up on the roofs and dropped heavy things onto them. They had ripped up shingles.

Bushes and shrubs were torn up. Stomped on.

Front doors were smashed in. Hacked to bits with axes.

Mailboxes were scattered along the street.

The only thing missing was graffiti. Probably because no one had spray paint. Or because it wasn't destructive enough. Who knew?

It looked like the work of particularly destructive teenagers.

And maybe it was.

It looked like the scene out of some post-apocalyptic movie.

But, in the movies, the world immediately turned into a scene like the one before them. In real life, it hadn't worked like that.

Sure, things had been destroyed. But sheerly by mistake. By accident. By chaos. Not on purpose.

And why had these homes been so pointlessly attacked, months and months after the EMP?

Terry didn't know, but his guess was that it had to do with the despair and rage that he himself felt. The others must have felt it as well. Maybe there'd been men and women who'd known their time was up, who'd known that they didn't have many days left. Maybe they'd had nothing, absolutely nothing, to direct their anger at. And then they'd come across those houses, standing there, like little reminders of the lives that they'd once had, or been promised.

"What's with all those houses?" said Sadie.

"Don't know," muttered Terry. "Not important."

"I thought you said we were almost there."

"We are."

"Are you lying?" There was some distrust in her voice.

Was she starting to suspect something was up?

No. It couldn't be. After all, he'd given her no reason to suspect anything.

They were extremely close to Terry's house.

"Of course I'm not lying, Sadie," said Terry. "See that over there?"

"What?"

"That big shed in that backyard?"

"Yeah."

"We're going to walk right past that. And then my house is across another long lawn. We're cutting through the backyards."

Sadie gave him a suspicious look.

"Well," said Terry. "I'm going. Either come with me, or I'll walk you back to your mom."

"No, I'm coming," said Sadie, picking up her pace again.

Terry smiled inwardly. Then became nervous again, while trying to hide it.

His brain was rapidly moving through plans.

Finally, he settled on one.

Terry's tired legs carried him in long strides, with Sadie following him, past the shed, and onto his property.

It was a little house. Out of the way of the vandals. Nothing fancy. Nothing spectacular. Nothing to attract any attention.

"They don't know you're coming," said Terry, pausing outside on the lawn. "I don't want to scare them."

"Scare them?" said Sadie. "I'm not going to scare anyone."

"We haven't had visitors in a long time," said Terry. "And that gun of yours might scare my daughter."

"She doesn't have a gun?"

"My wife didn't think it was a good idea. And we've done better with hiding than with fighting so far."

"I'll leave my gun outside," said Sadie.

It was clear in her eyes that she was desperate to meet Lilly.

Too bad that it'd never happen.

"Maybe that'd work," said Terry, feigning momentary confusion. "But let me just go inside and tell them you're coming. OK? Can you wait out here for a minute?"

"Of course," said Sadie, putting on a face that made her look ready to please.

"I'll be right back," said Terry. "Don't leave."

"I won't," said Sadie.

Terry turned his back and started walking towards his front door. Behind it, he knew his wife would be waiting.

Terry dug his key out of his pocket, but before he could put it in the lock, the door opened.

His wife's weary, emaciated face stared back at him. There were dark circles under her eyes.

She looked terrified. But she smiled.

"Olivia," he said. "Rope. Quickly. Get me some rope."

She didn't say anything. They had been through these kinds of tense moments before together. From experience, they both knew that the best way to survive was to simply provide the other with what they asked for. Or do what the other said.

She turned her back. A moment later, she turned back around, strong rope in her hands.

Terry grabbed it.

Now he had what he needed.

"Shut the door," he said.

Terry turned on his heel and marched back out the door, determination in his stride.

He could do this.

He needed to do this.

It was for his family. For his survival.

He was the man of the house, after all. He needed to set things right. No matter what it took.

10

MAX

ax had dozed off sometime after the sun had gone down. It hadn't been restful sleep. But instead a sleep punctuated with nightmares. Terrible dreams where Mandy had given birth to a beautiful baby girl. Only to have something unspeakably horrible happen to it.

He'd wake up, breathing heavy, feeling as if he'd just run a mile, with the intense darkness of the night around him. The clouds must have been heavy in the sky. The faint snores of his stockade companions.

He'd wake up and think of Mandy and wonder whether she was OK, whether she was eating right. He'd wonder what would happen to Mandy and the baby if he didn't return.

If Max had one quality that had helped him survive, it was that he never gave up. Somehow, he'd always pushed on. He'd always continued, no matter what the odds.

Max had always been able to ignore how he'd felt about a situation, ignore the mounting dread that the body and mind naturally produced in the face of difficult odds. He'd always been able to divorce himself from the fears that came up.

Others may have thought that he just hadn't felt fear. But it wasn't that. Fear was natural. Fear was everywhere. Fear was omnipresent.

It was what Max did with the fear that mattered.

But now? Now that he and Mandy were together? Now that there was a baby on the way? It was harder. So much harder.

He hadn't thought it would be. And now, faced with the reality that he couldn't process his dread and fear as well as he could before, he didn't know what to do.

Something that came easy to Max had suddenly become hard. That fact made it all seem so much more difficult.

He'd been asleep when the guard had come in. Given him a couple of swift kicks to wake him up, the pain intense and pumping through him.

He'd been dragged out of the stockade. Tossed to the ground like a rag doll, unable to fight back properly because of the pain. Another kick, this one harder.

Max lay on his side, involuntarily doubled over in the dirt.

He had no gun. No weapon. Even his watch had been taken from him.

He was weak from hunger. Weak from thirst. Weak from pain.

No matter how strong a man was, or thought he was, he could become nothing in the blink of an eye. He could become as weak as anyone. A couple of days without food would bring most men to their knees.

And most thought that they could deal with pain. But most hadn't experienced real pain.

Max looked up. A bright flashlight shone into his eyes.

He couldn't see much.

The light danced around. Max hoped for a glimpse of someone. His captors. Of his tormentors.

But he saw nothing. Not even a shadowy outline.

"Leave him with us. Back to your duties," said a harsh, deep voice. Gravelly. Male, definitely. Maybe early fifties. Late forties at the youngest.

It was the voice of a man who was used to getting what he wanted.

Then another voice. A familiar one. "What are you interested in him for? He's just a nobody. Came in today, arrogant as hell. Wanted a leadership role. Wouldn't take no for an answer."

Who was it? Where did Max know that voice from? His brain was sleepy. He wasn't putting things together properly.

"You think he's a nobody?" said the other voice, the gruffer voice, laughing harshly. "We'll see about that."

"How do you even know about him? I haven't even given you the nightly briefing. You don't have any of my reports from today." The familiar voice again.

Suddenly, Max realized who it was. It was Wilson. The man in the tent. The man with the paperwork. The man who had sent him to the stockade.

"I have my sources," said the gruffer voice. "I have eyes all around."

"And if he's not a nobody, Grant, just who is he?" said Wilson.

Grant! It was the man that Max had heard so much about. The leader himself. The famous Grant. The man who was going to restore order. The man who was going to stamp down chaos. The man for whom Max had, essentially, left his wife and unborn child for, thinking that he had the answers.

Well, maybe he still did.

"You remember the group that we had the most trouble with? Back about a month ago? All that fighting? We lost a lot of good men."

"The guys who called themselves the New Disorder? The anarchist group? The ones who welcomed the new chaos of the world and would stop at nothing to accelerate the spread of chaos, violence, and civil unrest. The ones who had hated civilization and society since who knows when."

"Exactly," said Grant. "You remember the leader?"

"The guy who called himself, improbably I might add, Moby Dick. Absurd name. Yes, I remember him. What about him?"

The pain was subsidizing a little bit for Max. He knew he shouldn't make a move. Not yet. Not before he knew what was going on. And what was going to happen to him.

But Max couldn't help himself. The fight was still in him.

Max moved. Just a little. Trying to see if he could get a look at Grant or Wilson. See what kinds of weapons they had.

Max's movement was ever so slight.

Grant didn't speak until after Max felt the pain. An incredible pain. Sharp and intense. It felt like a piece of metal had been smashed hard into his thigh.

"Don't move anymore," came Grant's stern voice. "Or you'll get it worse than that."

"Shit," muttered Wilson. "You don't want to break his leg, do you?"

The pain was bad.

But Max had felt worse.

"Maybe I do," said Grant.

"Just tell me what the hell's going on," said Wilson.

"What does a violent anarchist group have to do with this man here? Do you think he's one of them or something?"

"Nothing like that," said Grant.

"He's not one of them?"

"No."

"How do you know for sure? Maybe he is. Maybe this is a late-stage attack. An infiltration. Or a decoy. Something, anyway."

"He's not one of them," said Grant. "And I know because I talked to one of the leaders."

"One of the leaders? You talked to him? I thought they were all dead. We killed them all. Didn't we?" Wilson sounded more confused by the minute.

"Not all of them," said Grant. "I struck a deal with one of them."

"A deal?" Wilson couldn't have sounded more shocked.

"Exactly. A deal. It is what it is, and I won't apologize for it." He sounded vicious. Cruel. Intense. "In exchange for letting some of them live, I asked them to keep their ears to the ground. Provide me with information. They're in hiding now, their mission failed, but they still know people. They hear things."

"This is insane," said Wilson. "I just can't... you struck a deal like that... without consulting me..."

"Get over it," snapped Grant. "That's the way things are. I don't have time to consult everyone."

"I'm the second in command, though."

"Exactly. Second. I'm the first."

Wilson said nothing. It seemed as if he had no response.

Max opened his eyes again, to see if he could see again. Maybe the flashlight was now pointed off at an angle. But it wasn't. He was just hit with the blinding light, his eyes squinting reflexively

Max closed his eyes again before anyone noticed. Apparently Grant and Wilson were looking more at each other than at him. The conversation was getting intense.

Maybe Grant and Wilson would start fighting. A long shot, probably. But maybe. Just maybe.

If a fight broke out, Max would have a chance. A chance to escape.

Wilson seemed upset. Maybe angry. But probably not angry enough. He seemed too subservient. Too subservient to start fighting.

OK. A fight was a long shot. But if they weren't looking at him, maybe he had a shot now. Maybe he could escape. Break free. Run off.

Max wasn't bound. Seemed like a huge oversight.

Plans were quickly running through Max's head. He was trying to calculate angles, guessing where Wilson and Grant were from the sound of their voices.

It'd never work if they spotted him too early. Surely they were armed. They'd just shoot him in the leg or arm. Or the back, the bullet hitting his stomach. He'd bleed out slowly, and they'd try to get the information they wanted out of him then. It didn't seem like they'd care if he died or not.

But who did they think he was? It didn't make sense.

Apparently Wilson was wondering exactly the same thing.

"So who is he?" said Wilson. "He told me his name was Max. He told me he wanted to lead a local group, that he was interested in restoring order."

"Maybe his name is Max, for all I know," said Grant, his voice cold, emotionless. "Not that it matters. What I've learned from my anarchist contact..."

Wilson let out a long sigh, as if he was frustrated, as if he still simply couldn't fathom Grant dealing with an anarchist. But he said nothing, and Grant continued.

"There's another group like ours."

"Another group like ours? What do you mean?"

"Just what it sounds like. A militia composed of men and women of diverse background, many of them from the armed services, the police force, the government... all sorts of people who are interested in restoring order back to this great country."

"Another organization like ours? A group to fight the chaos? How is that possible? How haven't we heard of them?"

"They're based in California. Far away from us. They've grown very large. Larger, even, than our own camp here. And they're powerful, growing quickly, taking up new territories, slowly squashing the anarchism that had developed. That's why my anarchist contact was so interested in them. It was a serious threat to his desires for the world."

Wilson sounded stunned as he spoke rapidly in excitement. "A new organization... this is great news... it'll make our job so much easier... we'll team up with them... I've got to put together an envoy as soon as possible... this will speed up our plans for restoring order..."

"It'll never happen," said Grant.

"Never happen?"

"They'll swallows us up. They're at least ten times our size, by all estimates."

"OK..." said Wilson, clearly struggling to see the bigger picture. "So what? I'm sure we'll still get to our goal... we'll still be able to help... And anyway, what does this have to do with this man here?"

Max sighed internally. It was almost as if he could feel the eyes turning back onto him. He had been about to make his move. Now it was too late. Well, maybe they'd look away again.

The conversation seemed to be winding down. Grant seemed to be ready to make some point, to defy Wilson's expectations once and for all.

Max didn't know how this conversation would lead back to him. But he knew that when it did, it wouldn't be good. He had the sense something bad, something terrible, was about to happen to him. And he didn't want to wait around to find out what it was.

"This man," said Grant, "is a spy from the California militia. The anarchist told me one would come. He told me the day he'd arrive. He said that I needed to destroy him, or else face the consequences."

"Consequences? What the hell are you talking about? Clearly this anarchist was just feeding you a load of garbage. How would he know all this?"

Grant didn't answer him.

"What's your fear, anyway, here? Why are you so fixated on this other group? Our goal is to restore order. Get a government running again. Stop the violence and chaos. If that's their goal too, then everything should be fine, right?"

"I have no fear," said Grant. "But I will not let my leadership be challenged. As our own organization grows, I'll be the head of it. When we rule the whole country, I will rule..."

Wilson let out a little laugh. Kind of a half-scoff. It surprised Max. "So that's it, eh?" said Wilson. "You don't want to lose your big ego. You don't want to let your own power be challenged. I'm surprised at you, Grant, I thought better of you..."

A sudden sound, like a fist colliding with flash. Wilson suddenly let out a noise of pain. Then the sound of a body, likely Wilson's, collapsing heavily to the ground. Another grunt and groan of pain.

"I'll do what it takes," said Grant. "And I won't have anyone, even you, disrespecting me. When the time comes, we'll destroy this other militia. And I will reign over..."

Max thought it was now or never. He opened his eyes. A flashlight lay on the ground, pointing out into nothing. In the periphery of its beam, Max saw Wilson on the ground, clutching his stomach. Grant stood over him. A tall, muscular man. Powerfully built. An intense beard. Intense eyes.

Max scrambled to his feet.

"You egoistical bastard," spat Wilson.

Grant's foot lashed out. Fast. The toe of his boot collided with Wilson.

A grunt of pain.

Max had to make a split-second decision. Fight or flee.

It wasn't a matter of pride. Or ego. Neither of those mattered.

All that mattered was surviving. Whatever got the job done was the best option.

The choice was easy. Grant was almost certainly armed. And he was big enough and strong enough to make disarming him a serious problem.

Grant, in the flash impression that Max had, looked like he'd been eating well for a long time. Very well.

Max had been eating well. But not for that long. And only in comparison to how he'd been eating before they'd become stable, which wasn't very well at all.

Max was already turned the opposite direction.

His legs were moving under him. His mind was trying to get them to move fast. Very fast. But they were going slow. Felt like slow motion. Like he was stuck in quicksand.

Time had slowed down for Max. It was the adrenaline. It was everything, his whole mind and body painfully aware that this was really life or death.

And it was most likely going to be death.

At any moment, Max expected to feel pain. Then hear a gunshot. But he couldn't control that. He could just control how fast he ran.

His feet were pounding into the earth below him.

There were noises behind him. Heavy footsteps raining down. Heavy, fast breathing. The swish of arms through the air. And, farther back, the painful groans of Wilson.

The darkness was in front of him.

Then pain.

But no gunshot.

It wasn't a bullet wound.

Something had smacked into his leg. Something hard. Maybe metal or wood.

Max went tumbling, his leg giving out from under him. He fell forward, his fast pace propelling him into the darkness.

He broke his fall with his arms. But he fell hard, and his face smashed into the earth below him. Pain in his nose. The taste of blood. All normal. All almost routine.

Max knew he didn't have long. He pushed with his arms against the earth, twisting his body, trying to get so that he could at least face his attacker. He knew he didn't have time to get up. Not before Grant got to him.

Max got his body flipped over, his arms in front of him. He didn't have a weapon. But at least he could do something.

He would have never thought of doing nothing, of giving up. It wasn't in his character.

If it had been, he would have died long ago.

Grant was already there, waiting for Max to get himself flipped over. He looked tall in the shadows, in the darkness. His torso had that classic V-taper. Those classic broad, strong shoulders. It all seemed more pronounced in the harsh outlines of the darkness.

"You're going to tell me everything," growled Grant. "I'm not letting some halfwit Californian upstage me. Not after all this time. All this work I've put in."

Max didn't protest. He didn't open his mouth.

He'd do everything he could to survive.

But he wasn't going to protest his innocence. He wasn't that kind of man. This wasn't his kind of game.

Grant's fist was huge. It sped towards Max. Max's hands did nothing to block it.

Grant was strong. Very strong. His fist collided with Max's face.

Max's vision went fuzzy and black. Saw the bright lights scattered across the TV-like static.

Then another blow. And another.

The back of Max's head bounced off the earth underneath him. There was blood, and, somehow dirt, in his mouth.

"What's wrong with her?" whispered Cynthia.

"I don't know. Do you still have that book?"

"Book? Which book?"

"The midwife one. The one Max found at that old bookstore. Remember?"

Georgia was a little annoyed. Why did it sometimes seem like she had to explain everything?

"Be right back."

Mandy groaned in pain.

Cynthia slipped out the door. As she did, Georgia spotted John's worried face peering in.

"Go do something useful, John," snapped Georgia. "You're going to make us all nervous hanging onto our every word."

John gave a sheepish nod and his head disappeared again.

"I'm scared, Georgia," said Mandy.

Georgia was a mother, but she'd never been "that" type of mother exactly, the type that was good at showing caring, the type that was always sweet and knew how to show affection. Her own kids had said for years that she'd hardly ever hugged them, but that they'd known she'd cared for them because she'd have killed anyone who wronged her kids.

"It's going to be OK," said Georgia, patting Mandy in a somewhat artificial manner on her shoulder.

"You don't know that," said Mandy. "You're just saying that."

Most people would have denied it. Most people would have continued on, insisting that everything would definitely be OK, no matter what.

That wasn't Georgia's style.

"Things are looking bad," she said. "But not as bad as they could be. You're experiencing pain when you shouldn't. You're experiencing weakness when you shouldn't. You should be feeling good and strong, but you're not, and that's all a problem. And it'd all be fine if we had a hospital or a doctor. But we don't. We don't have much, except a book on midwifery."

"Midwife?" scoffed Mandy. "What good is that going to do me? Don't we have a real medical textbook somewhere?"

"Yes," said Georgia. "We do, but it's not going to do us a lot of good if all the solutions involve big fancy electric-powered machines that we simply don't have around. Midwifery, however, has existed for thousands of years and doesn't rely on things like that."

"It also can't cure many things," said Mandy. "If I've got a serious problem, I'll lose the baby. And I don't know if I can go through that. It'll be devastating."

"I'm not going to feed you a bunch of lines," said Georgia. "As you can see, I'm not good at that kind of stuff. I always say it like it is."

"That's why I can trust you."

"OK," said Georgia. "So here it is. If you lose the baby, it'll be devastating, but you'll get through it. But that's not the real danger."

"It's not?"

"The real danger is that you're far enough along in your pregnancy that you're not just going to lose the baby, but that we'll lose you as well."

Mandy's expression changed dramatically.

"Now," said Georgia. "We're going to do everything we can to stop that."

"How could you say that?" said Cynthia, appearing once again inside, her face full of fury. Fury directed right at Georgia. "You want to scare her to death or what?"

Georgia didn't know what to say. She did notice, however, that Cynthia had brought back the book she'd requested. The book on midwifery.

"Now don't worry, Mandy," said Cynthia. "Everything's going to be OK. Don't listen to Georgia. You're not going to die, and you're not going to lose the baby. We're not going to let that happen to you."

"Don't tell me things you don't know," said Mandy.

"I'm just trying to help. Unlike Georgia."

"At least she gives it to me straight."

"What's going on in there?" It was Dan's voice from outside the building.

"Everything's fine, Dan," called out Cynthia.

Georgia already had the midwife book open to the index. There was a list of pregnancy complications, as well as a short list of symptoms.

"I may have something," said Georgia, turning quickly to page 81, the short chapter for "back labor," which had some of the symptoms that Mandy had described. "Something called back labor... I don't know... I think I've heard of it before."

Georgia's own pregnancy was so long ago that she couldn't remember the various terms the doctors had used. She hadn't wanted, at the time, anything to do with midwives. She'd wanted doctors. Good old-fashioned doctors, and modern hospitals. It was funny that she was now looking at midwifery book, which, really, was a tradition far older than modern medical doctors, for better or for worse.

"Let me see the book," said Cynthia, trying to grab it from Georgia's hands. It was uncharacteristic of Cynthia, but the situation had everyone on edge, so maybe it was understandable.

"Just a minute," said Georgia, scanning the pages rapidly. "Shit. This is something that only happens during labor."

"Let me see it then," said Cynthia, sounding desperate. "I'm sure I'll find something."

"Mom?" It was James's voice from outside the building.

"Not now, James."

"This is serious."

"If your sister wants to work with you two, just let her," said Georgia, getting more annoyed and frustrated by the second.

"Sadie's gone," said James.

Georgia's heart felt like it stopped.

She snapped her head around.

James's head had appeared in the doorway. It wasn't the sort of thing James would ever joke about, not since the EMP, but after seeing his face, Georgia was 100 percent sure that he was serious. His young face looked weary, completely pale in color, as if the youth had been drained from it.

"Has anyone seen Sadie?" said Georgia, turning back to Cynthia.

"I already checked, Mom," said James. "I asked everyone."

"What about Mandy? She's been in here the whole time. Have you seen Sadie today, Mandy?"

Mandy's pained face shook back and forth. "No," she said. "Not since yesterday."

"Anyone else?"

Everyone was shaking their heads.

"Shit, shit," Georgia was muttering. "OK, James, when was the last time... we'll have to ask everyone..."

"Already did," said James. There was intense worry on his face. But also determination etched into it. And for that moment, despite Georgia's panic at losing her only daughter, she felt pride for James, pride in the fact that he already knew what to do. Obviously he cared about his sister, and he was smart and strategic enough to already have done everything he could do. Before even going to his mom, he'd asked everyone if they'd seen her, and thought about her last whereabouts.

"Where did you see her last?"

Before she could even get the sentence out, James was starting to answer. "This morning. Dan and I were planning our day's work, and we saw her drinking coffee. Then she was gone. We didn't think anything of it, but then she never showed up. Together we checked everywhere with a mile radius of the camp. She's not here."

"Shit."

Mandy let out a groan of pain.

There were two crisis situations coming at her from both fronts.

Georgia needed to think quick.

"OK," she said. "Cynthia, you stay here with Mandy. Do

what you can. Use the book as a reference but remember there's not much we're going to be able to do without medical equipment. If the pain gets bad, there's aspirin, and a wooden spoon for her to bite on. If you want to give her something else, make sure to check in the book to see if it is OK for pregnancy."

"But... she's going to be OK," Cynthia was saying.

"Good," said Georgia. "But if she's not, you're going to be here for her. John?"

"Yeah?" John's voice came outside the building.

"You're coming with me."

"Right," said John. He didn't need to ask what they were going to do. He already knew.

"Everyone else," said Georgia. "You're staying here."

"But, Mom! I've got to come..."

"They need you here, James. You and Dan are on permanent watch until I get back. John, get your gear together. Quick. Plenty of ammunition. Enough food for a couple days. But not too much. We're going to pack light and move fast."

Georgia gave Mandy and Cynthia a stiff nod that she hoped conveyed more than she knew how to say, then she was out of the building, moving through the darkness, headed towards her own gear.

It felt almost as if she had entered into a dream. She'd always done everything she could to protect her kids. And now this? It seemed unreal. It seemed as if it couldn't possibly be happening.

But it was. It had. Sadie was gone.

There wasn't any hope in not jumping to conclusions. Better to assume the worst than the best. Better not to be caught off guard.

If Sadie was still alive, wherever she was, Georgia would

find her. If Sadie wasn't still alive, which was a very real possibility, then whoever had done the act would pay. Pay dearly.

Georgia's heart was reacting, and her emotions, normally under control, were rearing their ugly head. But she managed to pack a bag. Food, water. Water filtration.

She already had her knives on her. Flashlights too.

She grabbed two rifles. Her favorites.

Plenty of ammunition.

An extra handgun.

One of the few working flashlights that still had batteries. Why it worked no one really knew. It was just one of those flukes. Maybe it had been housed in an accidental Faraday cage, protecting it from the EMP.

"You ready?" came John's voice.

"Just a second."

Georgia's eyes scanned the area rapidly, looking for anything she'd missed. No, nothing else to take. She wasn't the kind of woman who believed in having a lot of trinkets. She had no good luck charms or superstitions. If others believed in them, like Cynthia, that was fine. But they weren't for Georgia.

There wasn't time to say goodbye. There wasn't time to give any more instructions. There wasn't any time at all.

It was all happening so fast, and her mind was in such an unusual state, that it wasn't until Georgia and John were leaving camp, that Georgia realized they didn't know where to go.

They didn't have a clue where Sadie was. They didn't have a clue which direction she'd be in.

"We've got to pick one direction and just stick to it," said John.

"It's only a one-in-four shot," said Georgia, trying to keep her anger and panic under control. Her face felt red and hot. She tried to focus on her breathing. In and out. In and out.

"Worse than that," said John. "It's not like she's going to be due east."

"Shit," exclaimed Georgia suddenly, slamming her foot hard into a tree trunk out of sheer anger and frustration. Pain shot through her foot. It was uncharacteristic of her, doing something pointless that hurt herself. But it just seemed so hopeless. She wanted to just open her mouth wide and scream.

But she didn't. She kept it under control. She kept it bottled down.

"There's got to be something we can do," said John. "Somewhere we can look. Somewhere nearby. Where would you take someone if you kidnapped them?"

"I wouldn't kidnap anyone."

"If you had to."

"The woods. Away from everyone."

"OK. But that's you, Georgia. You're not most people. You're not exactly normal. And that's good. It's what makes you effective. But what about your average person? Your average kidnapper?"

"What would they want to kidnap a kid for anyway?" said Georgia.

John shrugged. It was clear he didn't want to answer her. The possibilities were all too terrible.

"I think your average idiot kidnapper would take the kidnappee somewhere fairly close by. Sadie's a tough cookie, regardless of her age. She's going to be hard to take real far."

"Well, they took her. She's missing."

John had a look on his face like didn't want to say what he was thinking. And Georgia didn't ask him. She didn't have to. She knew that they were assuming the best-case scenario. Kidnapping was the best- case scenario. Death was the worst.

For all they knew, Sadie could be lying dead somewhere just outside the area that James and Dan had already checked. Or she could be just dead, or dying, under a pile of dead leaves. After all, it'd be impossible to check every actual square inch of the surrounding forest.

Georgia had to make up her mind. And fast. There wasn't any more time to waste on her decision.

She had to go with her gut feeling. Ignore all her thoughts. Ignore John.

"We'll head to the shopping mall. The one on I-5. There's a chance she's there. Max told me he came across some lowlifes around those parts."

John hesitated, before nodding in agreement.

And with that, they were off, each one trying to keep up with the other. The pace was fast. Very fast. And it had to be.

Georgia's thoughts were racing. There was no calming her mind. Not now. Not with what had happened.

12

SADIE

Something wasn't right.

Sadie's suspicion was rising. It had been nonexistent before.

Had she been blinded by her enthusiasm for making a friend, for finding someone her own age to play with?

But now, as she stood outside Terry's house, and watched his back, she wondered why she'd had to wait outside. And what was Terry talking to his wife for?

Was Sadie really that much of a threat? Sure, she was an outsider, but she was just a child. She knew that she wasn't big or scary.

Her gun was in her hands again. It felt good there. Just in case something happened, it was good to know she had it.

The safety was off. Her finger was near the trigger. Not quite pressing it. But inside the trigger guard.

Her heart was pounding. Anxiety. Anticipation. Adrenaline, causing a slight shaking in her hands.

She took a deep breath. Held it to the count of three. Let it out. Did it all again. Her hands felt a little better. A little steadier.

Should she leave?

She had just seconds to decide.

Yes. She needed to get out of here. Her gut was clenched up. Her body was reacting, telling her this wasn't right.

But maybe it was just nerves. Maybe it was just anxiety that meant nothing, like when she'd almost thrown up before giving a school report in front of the class, only to have it all work out fine in the end.

Shit. What should she do?

She started to turn around, getting ready to run off, but before she'd turned ninety degrees, she saw Terry himself turning around.

There was something in his hands. What was it?

Rope.

There was rope in his hands.

Why was there rope in his hands?

There was a strange look on his face. A strange look in his eyes.

He was moving fast. Long strides. Headed right towards Sadie.

He hadn't closed the door behind him, and in the doorway, his wife stood and looked out, watching Terry, and glancing up at Sadie. Her expression was inscrutable. Something was going on, but it was impossible to tell what.

Sadie raised her gun.

"What's up, Sadie?" said Terry, not ceasing to continue walking towards her.

"You tell me what's up. What's that rope for?"

"The rope? Oh, nothing."

Sadie said nothing. Just gritted her teeth. Finger pressing ever so slightly against the trigger. Muzzle of the gun aimed squarely at Terry's chest.

"Why don't you put the gun down, Sadie?"

"I don't trust you."

"Well, that makes sense. We just met. But I thought we were getting along."

"Tell me what the rope's for, and maybe I'll put the gun down. If you wanted to attack me, you're going to need more than rope, anyway."

"Attack you?" Terry let out a weary little laugh that sounded a little less than genuine.

Maybe Sadie was overreacting to all this. Maybe she was just paranoid. Maybe she had spent too long cooped up in the woods trying to survive with the others. Maybe all her normal social impulses had been inverted, completely changed around.

"My wife just wanted me to tie it up in the tree over there, so that you and Lilly can swing on it. I'll stay outside with you two and make sure everything's OK."

Sadie didn't know what to say. The idea of playing on a tree, swinging on a rope, was too strange, too foreign, and too tempting.

"Where's Lilly?"

"Oh, she'll be right out. She just wanted to change into some better clothes in order to meet you. She hasn't been able to wear her favorite stuff, since it all gets worn out."

Sadie looked down at her own clothes, which were dirty, stained, and worn out. She felt embarrassed about them.

Terry was close to her now. There hadn't been much space between them to cross, and he had talked through most of it.

Slowly, Sadie had lowered her gun. Lowered her defenses. After all, Terry wasn't trying to hurt her? He would have done it earlier. There'd been endless opportunities. Sadie had just been working herself up into a panic.

"Lilly will be right out," said Terry, with a single glance back towards his wife in the doorway.

Then, suddenly, his strong adult hands had grabbed Sadie's arms.

What was going on? He was attacking her?

Sadie struggled, pushing back against him. But he was too strong, and she was strong, but she was just a kid. She was no match for him.

Terry moved, shifted so that one of his hands grabbed both her wrists. He was strong enough and his hand was big enough that he could do it.

His other free hand, dropping the rope, went to grab the handgun that was still in her hand. It was pointing harmlessly towards the sky.

No words were spoken. But Sadie glanced at his eyes, which hadn't changed. There was no evil glimmer that had come on all of a sudden. There was just the same look as there had always been. He was the same man as before; he'd just tricked her. The only thing new in his expression was determination.

Sadie wasn't going to let him take the gun. Without it, she had no chance.

She gritted her teeth, and, with all her strength, pushed her one arm back against his hand. She did it suddenly, her force catching Terry somewhat off guard. He let the push shift his own arms, and now her handgun was pointed at Terry.

He wouldn't let it point at him long.

It was just one instant. The barrel almost against his stomach, due to how much shorter Sadie was.

There wasn't going to be time to try to get a different shot. And, why did she need one? The stomach was fine.

Sadie didn't hesitate at all. She pulled the trigger.

The gun kicked.

Her ears rang.

Terry grunted strangely, an odd look appearing on his face. A look of surprise. Of something else. Something she couldn't read.

His hands let go of Sadie, and she pulled herself free.

But she didn't move much. She only took one step back, and stood there, stunned, looking at Terry.

"What have you done?" Terry's wife's voice rose to a high pitch, in terror and shock, with the noise barely rising above the intense ringing in Sadie's ears. She was rushing from the doorway towards Terry, who was slowly sinking to his knees, clutching his stomach.

A spot of blood was growing on his dingy and tattered shirt, over his emaciated abdominal area.

Sadie knew that a wound like that to the stomach meant death. A slow, painful death.

Terry's wife had nearly reached Terry and Sadie. It was a toss-up, whether she'd go to comfort Terry, or whether she'd attack Sadie. There was no reason in Sadie's mind that she should trust Terry's wife.

Sadie pointed her gun at Terry's wife. "Stop!" she shouted.

Sadie didn't want to shoot someone else. She didn't want to kill this woman.

But, then again, she didn't want any of this life.

This was what she had.

And she, like her mother, knew that she was going to survive. No matter what. No matter how many people she had to kill.

"Don't shoot!" The woman raised her hands above her hand. A look of terror on her face, and in her eyes, which darted between Sadie and Terry.

Terry had sunk down completely to the ground, lying on his side, his eyes staring up to the sky.

The woman's eyes kept bouncing back and forth between Sadie and Terry. And, then, all of a sudden, they flitted back to the house that she'd come out of.

Sadie's eyes followed too. She wanted to see what the woman was looking at. Was there someone else in the house? Another threat.

That's when Sadie saw the girl, about her age, standing in the doorway where, not long before, her mother had been.

The sight was strange. Unexpected. So there really was a girl her age. A girl she could have been friends with, had things been different.

But they weren't different.

Sadie's eyes lingered on the girl for too long.

Suddenly, something smacked into her head. Something hard. Her vision went momentarily black. She lost her balance, started to fall, but caught herself at the last moment.

Sadie's eyes, turning back, saw the woman. Terry's wife was standing over her, a piece of hardwood in one hand. Her eyes glared at Sadie.

"You shot my husband," she snarled. "You'll pay for this."

Sadie was dizzy. It was hard to concentrate on the gun. But she started to raise it.

But before she could get the gun aimed again, the woman swung the wood again.

This time, the wood hit Sadie's shoulder. Hard. Felt harder than the blow to her head.

Sadie lurched from the blow. After all, she didn't weigh much. Not nearly as much as an adult. She was no match for the adult woman. Unless she could get the gun straight.

"The gun," groaned Terry. "Get the gun."

Strong adult hands on the gun. Female hands. Sadie felt it being wrenched from her own hands.

Now she was helpless. No gun.

Now the strong female hands were at her neck. Squeezing. Hard.

Sadie tried to gasp. But she couldn't.

There was no air.

She couldn't breathe.

Was this going to be how it ended?

For a long time, she'd thought she'd go down from a bullet. And then, for a time, it seemed as if starvation would do her and her family in.

But being strangled by a woman, by a mother? She'd never thought it would end this way.

The hands were getting tighter.

Sadie simply couldn't breathe at all. She wouldn't last long.

Images started to flash through her mind's eye. Images of her younger years, not so long ago. Memories of times that had been lost, times from before the EMP.

"Don't... kill..." It was Terry's voice, croaking out a couple words. "Need... alive..."

Suddenly, the hands loosened. The grip relaxed.

Sadie gasped.

Air came rushing in.

"She's done you in, Terry. Don't you realize that?" There was anger in the woman's voice. Intense anger. Anger and pain. She knew she was going to lose her husband. She knew that there was nothing she could do, that there was no way she could patch up the wound. No way to save him.

Sadie lay there on her back, weak, like a fish gasping for air, listening.

Terry spoke slowly, his words weak, his voice full of intense physical pain. Sadie remembered hearing that there was no more painful way to go out than being shot in the stomach. Maybe it was true and maybe it wasn't. Either way, it probably didn't feel good.

"We... need... her... alive... she's... daughter.... group that... has... everything... group in the... woods... use her as... hostage... get what you... need for after... I'm gone."

The woman was crying now. Audibly.

Sadie, still gasping for breath, was trying to get to her feet. She was scanning the ground, looking for the gun that she had lost. She needed to fight back. She wasn't going to let this happen.

"So that was your plan, Terry? Use this girl as a hostage? That's what was going to keep us alive? You coward..." The woman's' crying was louder now. Intense. "I guess I have no choice now. Now that you've gone and gotten yourself killed through your idiocy and cowardliness; you've left me in an awful position. The position of having to follow through on your plan since I have nothing else to do, no other way to protect myself and Lilly."

Suddenly, the woman was on top of Sadie, pushing her against the ground. The woman's strong hands pinned Sadie down as she used the rope that Terry had brought over.

Sadie tried to fight back. But the woman was too strong and easily overpowered her.

Soon, Sadie's wrists and ankles were tightly bound with thick rope.

Sadie lay on her back, unable to move, except to wiggle, staring up at the sky. Completely useless Completely powerless.

Somewhere, unseen by Sadie, Terry groaned in pain.

"I don't like this any more than you do," said the woman. "But this is the situation my idiot husband put us in. So you're my hostage. Don't blame me. I'm just trying to survive. You'll understand when you're older. Now, who are your parents, and where are they? I don't think my husband thought this through very well, but I'm going to have to let them know somehow that I have you hostage..."

The woman's face suddenly appeared above Sadie's, blocking out the sky.

The woman asked again. "Who are they?"

Sadie spat in the woman's face. A huge glob of spit.

She'd never give up her family that easily.

But, unfortunately, Terry, if he didn't die first, would be able to tell his wife exactly what to do, whatever his plan had been. And, in all likelihood, he'd live for a good number of hours before he finally bit the dust.

13

MAX

The blows rained down on Max. His body quivered in pain. His body was so full of pain that it became pain.

If he'd been able to think a single normal thought, it would have been that what he hated most of all was simply not being able to fight back. The pain wasn't the hardest thing for him to deal with. It was the lack of agency. The lack of taking action.

Max's mouth was somehow full of dry earth. It felt horrible in his mouth. Dry. Disgusting. It hit the back of his throat. His face was pressed into the dirt now. A boot pressed hard down on his back. He felt the pain in his spine radiating up towards his skull.

Another boot came down hard, right onto his shoulder blade.

Max couldn't help it. He let out a scream of pain. Dry. As if the saliva was gone from his mouth.

For so long, Max had been searching for an answer. He'd been searching for someone or something to bring order out of chaos. From what he'd heard, the man who could do it was Grant.

Max had thought he'd needed to find Grant. To talk to him. To work for him.

And he'd finally found him.

He'd found Grant.

The same man who was kicking him. The same man who was inflicting so much psychical pain. The same man who was about to kill him.

Max had found what he'd thought he needed, only to discover that he'd needed something else entirely all along.

Max should have never left Mandy. Never left his unborn child. Never left the camp.

He should have never come.

And now he'd never get a second chance.

It was a hell of a way to go out. After everything that he'd avoided, all the danger he'd fought through, he'd finally dug his own grave by marching right into the lion's den. Max only had himself to blame. He'd delivered himself right to Grant.

The boots were off Max's back now. No pressure. No weight.

Max could move. He shifted his weight around, bending his knee, pushing with his hand against the ground. He was going to get up. He was going to fight. Maybe he wouldn't live, but at least he'd go down fighting.

But before Max could get up, another boot smashed into his side, sending him collapsing back to the ground, letting out a grunt of pain.

"I thought you were the type of man who'd let me get up to fight," said Max, laboriously, through gritted teeth. His breathing was heavy and labored. It was difficult to speak through the pain.

"I'm the type of man who knows not to give his enemies any chance," growled Grant.

Another boot smashed into Max. This time into his face.

Max felt the pain. His lip burst open. More blood in his mouth. Pain in his cheek. Deep in it. A couple of teeth loose. Tumbling around his mouth. More blood. More pain.

"This'll be better with... using my own two hands," growled Grant.

Max was on his back, lying in the dirt. Struggling to get up.

In a flash, Grant sank to his knees. His knees, like sharp points, dug into Max's belly and chest.

Max couldn't breathe. Just a little bit. Just a little air coming through. Like trying to breathe through a plugged-up straw while on the bottom of the ocean.

Two rough strong hands were around Max's neck. Squeezing. Hard. Very hard.

Now Max really couldn't breathe.

This was it. This was really it.

Partial images flashed through Max's mind.

Childhood memories. Images of Mandy. Strange, partial thoughts, neither coming nor going.

"Good riddance," growled Grant.

Grant's face was right up against Max's, as if Grant wanted to see Max die in an up close and personal way.

Max stared right back, right into Grant's eyes. Beads of sweat formed on Grant's forehead and dripped down onto Max's face.

Grant stank, a horrible stench that went right into Max's nostrils. The smell of an animal, the smell of rot and the smell of the death that would come soon enough.

A noise behind Grant. Like a twig snapping.

Without releasing his hold on Max's neck, Grant turned his head partway around.

But it wasn't enough.

Max saw it. Up close and personal. He saw the huge hard stick swinging right towards Grant's face. He saw Grant try to avoid it. He saw Grant try to duck.

Max saw the stick smack into Grant's face.

Max felt the strong hands release. It happened suddenly.

Max gasped for air, suddenly able to breathe.

Grant's eyes rolled back. A funny look came over Grant's face as he started to slide down to the side. Grant slid right off Max.

As Grant's body slid away, it revealed the man who'd been standing behind Grant. The man who'd swung the stick. The man who'd saved Max's life.

It was Wilson. The same man who'd thrown Max in the stockade earlier.

Wilson looked tall there in the darkness. Tall and thin. A strange sort of strength about him. A grim expression on his face.

Wilson extended a long arm down, his hand reaching towards Max.

Max was sputtering, still gasping. But he knew he didn't have time to waste. Or options. He grabbed Wilson's hand.

Wilson pulled Max to his feet.

"We've got to get out of here," said Wilson. He spoke quickly. Urgently.

"No shit," Max managed to say, despite coughing, his neck killing him.

Wilson's hand disappeared for a moment, dipping down into an unseen holster. Reappeared with a handgun.

Max nodded at Grant, who lay unconscious in the dirt in

the darkness. The gesture was asking a question. The question was: why don't you shoot Grant?

There were footsteps off in the darkness. Probably the penitentiary guard coming running.

There wasn't much time.

Wilson pointed off into the darkness, in a direction away from the stockade.

Max realized he'd have to verbalize the question. Better to make it a statement. "Shoot him. Kill Grant."

It was painful to speak. Painful to get the words out.

Wilson gazed down at Grant. There was some kind of internal debate happening inside his head.

Max could hazard a guess. Grant was Wilson's superior. But Wilson was having trouble with some new revelations about Grant. Not to mention being attacked by him.

Max knew Grant needed to die. Right then and there. Or else Grant would come back to haunt them.

If Grant lived, they weren't going to get very far. They weren't going to live for very long. Not with Grant alive and an entire militia camp at his orders.

The footsteps were thudding. Nearby. Very close.

Max wasn't armed. So he reached down, fumbling around Grant's unconscious body, looking for the holster.

Found it. His hand grasped Grant's handgun. Got it out of the holster.

Max raised it. Couldn't see the manufacturer in the darkness. But he could feel the weight of the gun. Felt for the safety. Found it.

"I'll do it myself," said Max.

Max pointed the gun at Grant's unconscious body.

"Don't," said Wilson, pointing his gun at Max.

"We've got to. He'll come after us."

"You shoot him," said Wilson. "You die. If you don't, you have a chance of living."

Max couldn't argue. The terms were clear. And Wilson's face showed no signs that he wasn't completely serious.

The footsteps were louder. The guard was near. Very near.

Max caught a glimpse of the guard in the darkness, raising a long gun.

Max reacted quickly, pointing his handgun over Wilson's shoulder, at the guard.

Max pulled the trigger. Twice. In quick succession, before Wilson could react.

Max saw the surprise on Wilson's face. He heard the shots. Then realized that he wasn't dead or shot.

Wilson turned his head, saw the dead guard.

"Come on," said Max. "I assume they'll send more. Not killing Grant is a mistake, and you know that better than I do."

"It is what it is," said Wilson, who took off at a run, heading in the opposite direction of the stockade.

Max took one last look at Grant's unconscious body and took off running after Wilson.

Max knew it was a mistake not to kill Grant. A huge mistake.

But at least he was alive.

His leg was hurting worse than usual. He could taste blood. His whole body hurt. As he ran, another tooth came loose, and Max spat it out without a second thought.

They were running side by side now, heading into the darkness.

Behind them, alarms sounded. Mechanical alarms. All sorts of non-electronic sounds were coming at them. Pots and pans banging. Gongs. Whistles. Shouts and yells. People hollering.

"They're not going to give us much of a head start," said Wilson.

Max didn't bother wasting his breath. After being beaten by Grant, it was hard enough to keep up with Wilson.

Wilson's decisions didn't make sense to Max. Why was he doing this? Why was he risking his life? Had he gone off his rocker? Had he been so offended that his boss had attacked him that he'd simply lost his cool and decided to go on the run?

"We've got to take a break, Georgia," said John.

"Not yet. Just a little bit farther."

They'd been walking at a swift pace all night. Georgia had refused to stop even to take a drink of water or eat a snack to keep her going. Instead, she'd made them consume their food and water as they walked, never resting, not even for a moment.

John simply didn't know what to say to Georgia. He didn't know how to comfort her. He knew that Georgia wouldn't stand for it, anyway. She wouldn't like hearing false words of comfort.

After all, there was no reason that John could come up with to be optimistic about the situation.

Finding Sadie was a long shot. They were headed to the shopping area. But why did they think Sadie might be there? No reason, really. Except that some bad people had been hanging out there. And they might end up there again. They might have taken Sadie there.

But it really didn't make any sense.

Then again, there weren't any other options. There wasn't anything to go on.

That's what happened these days when someone disappeared. There were cell phones. No way to track them. No police force to call to get on the case. No detectives to track anyone down. No private eyes. Nobody to help.

Just a distraught, angry mother, and her friend, stomping along down the road in the middle of the night.

Hopefully they didn't come across anyone that wanted a fight. Because, those that were still alive these days knew something about surviving. They either knew how to stay out of the way or they knew how to fight. And win.

And winning meant killing.

The farther they got from the EMP, the more dangerous the individuals remaining were. It was Darwin's theory at work. To the extreme.

Georgia was panting from exertion. So was John.

"I can't keep this up," said John. "'Member what Max is always telling us? And you too, for that matter."

"What?" snapped Georgia.

"That we're not going to be any good in a fight if we're completely exhausted. Pushing ourselves too far doesn't do us any good. Or Sadie. What if we find her, and can't rescue her because we've simply walked too far?"

Georgia said nothing, but she clearly reorganized that John had a good point, because she stopped in her tracks.

John stopped too.

"Come on," he said. "Let's get a little off the road. We're out in the open here."

The sun was starting to come up. Dawn was approaching. And that meant that it'd be more dangerous to be out and about. They'd be more visible. Easier to spot. Easier to shoot. Easier to pick off by one means or another.

They found a little spot off the road, near an empty parking lot, with some bushes and trees around for cover.

John took food and water out of his pack and handed it to Georgia.

"Why don't you sit down?" said John. "It's hard to rest when you're still on your feet."

He had to actually put a hand on Georgia's shoulder to get her to sit down cross-legged.

"Don't worry," he said. "I'll keep standing. Keep a lookout. All that."

She just nodded silently and ate her pemmican, taking sips of her water.

John didn't know what to say. Nothing came to mind that didn't sound stupid or insulting or downright insensitive.

John didn't think the chance of finding Sadie were good. In fact, they were downright terrible.

How could they expect to leave camp, head in one direction and find her when there were 360 other points around the circle of the camp that they could have departed from as well?

Their plan didn't make much sense. And John assumed Georgia knew that.

The initial excitement and adrenaline rush seemed to be wearing off. Georgia had been all geared up, ready to go find her daughter. Now they'd been walking all night and they were tired. Now the plan seemed even more pointless. Now it seemed as if they might just walk endlessly, never finding anything.

John didn't know what to do. They couldn't just give up before they started. They couldn't just let Sadie disappear into nothing. They couldn't just forget her. It simply wasn't going to happen.

They couldn't let her just vanish with a trace. Without retribution.

But John also knew that if he and Georgia just simply continued walking for days and days, never finding Sadie, they'd eventually run into some sort of trouble.

Sure, it was safer to be out these days than it had been several months ago. Safer in the sense that there were fewer people. But more dangerous in plenty of other ways.

And danger would always be there. If they continue on and on, they'd eventually meet their own demise. No matter how prepared they were, no matter how hard they fought, if they continuously exposed themselves to danger, they'd eventually die.

That's just the way it was.

John held his tongue. He realized that his thoughts were getting ahead of himself. Way ahead.

They weren't at great risk yet. At least he didn't think so. They weren't that far from camp.

If it kept up for a week, and Georgia was intent on continuing, maybe then he'd have to talk to her. Until then, he was with her 100 percent.

John's thoughts shifted, and he started wondering whether they'd made the right decision in heading to the commercial center.

Maybe they should have stayed closer to the camp, circling around and around, making concentric circles with their tracks.

"What's that?" said Georgia, interrupting John's wandering, tired thoughts.

"I don't hear anything."

"Shut up and listen."

Georgia set aside her water bottle, grabbing her rifle instead.

John knew well enough to take Georgia's advice seriously. So he shut up and listened.

He didn't hear anything for a full half a minute, but he patiently waited. Meanwhile, he got himself ready for a fight.

Georgia, for all her practically minded traits, did have her quirks. And she was stubborn enough not to ever hint at changing them. For instance, she insisted on using one of her old hunting rifles, when something more modern would have been more appropriate, especially for a mission like this.

Then again, who was John to tell her what worked better for her? They were, after all, her own preferences. And it was her own daughter on the line.

John, instead, had brought along an AR-15. Solid and reliable. A good, serious weapon.

John, still unable to hear anything, was moving his eyes up and down the road.

It was empty. Just nothing but pavement. No cars. No people. Nothing.

Maybe Georgia was more tired than she was letting on. Exhausted to the point of hearing things, maybe.

Then he heard it.

A low, rumbling sounding engine

"Shit," he muttered.

They hadn't heard or seen a working vehicle in a long time. He didn't know how long.

There were some vehicles that had somehow survived the EMP. Probably because they were older, and had fewer electronics systems incorporated into their workings. Those that had survived the EMP, though, had, at this point, probably broken down. They'd come across vehicles themselves that would start up but had simply broken down mechanically in ways that they were unable to fix.

The final problem, and the most dire one, was that of fuel. It was hard to get fuel. That was the reality. It could be potentially taken out of gas stations, or siphoned from other vehicles, but there were so many people interested in doing that, not to mention hoarding gasoline, that it had already become quite scarce.

John and everyone else had given up on having a working vehicle of their own. Better to just walk. Not to mention safer. Easier to hide out.

"We need to get back more," hissed Georgia, in a low voice. "Better hidden."

John nodded his agreement. And, in fact, he couldn't agree more. He didn't like the low rumbling sound that was growing louder now by the second.

Georgia must have had much better hearing than he did, since she'd heard it so much earlier. John knew that she'd been careful to wear ear protection whenever she'd practiced at the range, before the EMP.

Now, there was no such thing as ear protection. They fired their guns when they needed to, not caring about their hearing.

And, for some reason, Georgia's seemed to have held up better than John's, he, who'd never fired a gun before in his life before the EMP had hit and had finally realized the importance of firearms.

It wasn't good to know that his hearing was partially shot. Or not as good as it could have been.

But it was even worse to know that some kind of vehicle was coming in their direction.

Together, they scrambled back farther away from the road. They kept low, crouching down.

There wasn't really anything that would completely hide them. The trees weren't thick enough, even at the bases of the trunks.

So they had to settle for getting down on their bellies, hoping that the trees and the distance would help to keep them covered.

John glanced over at Georgia briefly as he tried to get himself set up properly. She was a natural, her rifle somehow always in a good position.

He, on the other hand, had to shuffle and fiddle, trying to get it just right, where the gun didn't seem to dig into him, where the kickback wouldn't injure him.

They didn't have long to wait.

The rumbling was louder.

Soon enough, there it was. They could see it.

It looked improbable. Strange. A weird sight. Almost surreal.

It was a large army transport vehicle. It looked ancient, or at least modern in any sense.

It was the kind of truck that you might spot in an old Korean War movie.

It trundled along slowly, inching down the road.

It was moving slowly enough that a man could walk alongside it at a quick pace.

And, in fact, there were men walking alongside it. And in front of it. And behind it.

John counted six men, all with long guns. They didn't march like they were in the army, but they walked in a purposeful way, their heads moving so that their eyes could survey the surroundings.

The men wore all sorts of clothes. Tattered jeans. Flannel shirts. T-shirts. Work shirts. Half-torn-up dress shirts.

They all had long hair that hadn't been washed.

Some of them had the odd piece of camo-style gear, but not many of them.

The sight reminded John of stories of the old covered-wagon days, where the wagon would carry the supplies and some of the people, while others walked alongside it. Once in a while, when someone got tired, they'd hop on in the wagon, and someone else would hop out so that they could stretch their legs.

John couldn't see what was inside the army transport truck, but he figured it had to be something. Not to mention at least a few more men.

Those six men could have walked along that road on their own just fine. The truck wasn't doing them any favors, except maybe to carry their food.

So there had to be some reason that truck was there. Maybe it carried something important, or maybe it had a job to do somewhere else, where it was needed.

Either way, John didn't like the looks of it. It stank of organization. Organized force, organized power. But not the good kind.

Hopefully, the men would be concerned mainly with guarding their truck and whatever it contained. Hopefully, they wouldn't be looking for trouble.

So far, so good. The men hadn't spotted them.

The truck had traveled about half the distance of the visible road that lay stretched out in front of John and Georgia.

The men, it seemed, worked and walked mainly in silence. No one spoke. No orders were issued. No commands were shouted.

John glanced over at Georgia.

Her face showed no emotion. It was completely impassive. Her eyes watched the men, but other than that there was no movement.

John glanced back at the truck and the men.

Then it happened.

One of the men turned, as if he had heard something.

Turned in John's direction.

At first, the man seemed to be looking at something behind John, even though John had heard nothing.

What was the man looking at?

John tried to press himself further into the ground. It was just instinct. He knew that it was useless. He couldn't make himself disappear, no matter how hard he tried.

He and Georgia shouldn't have been spotted. But if someone were looking right in their direction, then they'd be seen.

John held his breath. Out of fear. Out of anxiety.

After all, Georgia could shoot well. She could fight. And John was no slouch. Not with the experiences he'd been through. And with Georgia's and Max's training.

But two against six? And possibly more?

No way.

It wasn't going to work

It wasn't going to happen.

They'd die.

If those guys wanted a fight, that was.

Maybe they didn't want a fight.

John and Georgia would just have to wait and see what happened.

The man still seemed to be looking at something behind John. At what? A tree? An animal? Another person?

Then the man's head snapped back down and around, his eyes fixating right on John.

The man barked an order, inaudible over the rumbling of the military truck.

John's eyes scanned the men rapidly. They were moving into some kind of position, some kind of formation, as if they'd done this all before.

The truck stopped, but the engine kept rumbling.

No shots fired.

Not yet, anyway.

John glanced at Georgia. What would she want them to do?

Fight or flee. That was always the question.

Still no shots fired.

Why hadn't they just shot them?

But the men were moving out towards John and Georgia, taking slow, plodding steps. They were now in a line. Their weapons were drawn. Their eyes peeled. Their heads scanning.

The sight reminded John of a search party, when volunteers would get together and comb the woods for a body.

It was all very strange.

What kind of fighting position was this?

Why hadn't they just shot at John when the man had spotted him?

Georgia turned to him. "Get ready," she hissed. "We're running. After I fire."

"Wait, what? You're going to shoot?" whispered John, as quietly as he could. "Shouldn't I...?"

"No," hissed Georgia, her voice firm and commanding. "Run after I fire. Get ready. I'm shooting in five seconds."

The message was clear. John was to do as he was told. He didn't understand the logic himself right now, but that didn't mean it wasn't there.

He shifted his body, trying to position himself so that he could get up quickly.

This didn't make sense.

Wouldn't they just shoot them as soon as they popped up? Especially after Georgia shot one of them.

It seemed like a suicide mission.

It seemed like a horrible plan. A horrible idea.

John trusted Georgia, but did he trust her this much?

G rant opened his eyes to sunlight peeking in
through the rudimentary window.

It was early morning.

His head hurt. Throbbing pain. A splitting headache.

Other parts of his body hurt, but his head was foggy and he couldn't identify what they were.

For a second, Grant didn't know where he was.

His mind jumped to conclusions.

Had he been kidnapped? Taken hostage? Someone intent on capturing the great leader of the most powerful militia on the East Coast?

Maybe.

Maybe not.

Then he saw it.

Something moving outside the window. It was a tree. A tree he'd seen before, its branches gently swaying in the breeze.

Then it came to him in a flash, and he realized where he was.

Grant was in the infirmary.

He turned his head, looking around.

He was in a rudimentary hospital bed, probably scavenged by one of his reclamation teams.

There was an IV running out of his arm up to a clear plastic bag. Some kind of saline solution, probably.

The militia wasn't short on supplies, not even hospital supplies. And it was all thanks to Grant's own initiative, sending teams out to scout the areas both far and near, searching for anything that could be useful.

"Nurse!" snapped Grant, his voice loud and commanding.

A flurry of tiny footsteps in the hallway. Someone was scurrying towards him.

Two heads popped in, appearing in the doorway.

A man and a woman.

Both nurses.

He recognized them as nurses. Real trained professionals from before the EMP.

They weren't messing around here at the militia camp. Grant wouldn't have stood for anything less than the real thing. He'd made sure that the nurses were real, that the equipment was as good as they could get it without electricity, and that there was even one real doctor.

"How are you feeling?" The woman snuck through the doorway and into the room. She acted as if she were doing something wrong, as if she shouldn't be there. She walked with a bit of a stoop, hunched over, her eyes downcast.

Grant understood well what was going on here. She was scared of him. And the male nurse was too.

Good. They had good reason to be scared of Grant.

"What happened?" barked Grant.

He needed answers. He needed them fast.

The last thing he could remember was that Wilson had betrayed him.

That bastard. After all Grant had done for him.

Grant would get him.

Grant wouldn't tolerate threats to his authority, whether internal or external. He'd squash them the way he'd always squashed them.

Wilson had served him well for a long time, but it was clear that he wasn't the man Grant thought he was.

It didn't matter, though. Wilson had done his job. There'd be another man to fill his place.

Knowing what he now knew, that Wilson was nothing more than a common traitor, Grant was glad that he hadn't kept Wilson informed of everything.

He was glad that he'd kept Wilson in the dark about Grant's more ambitious projects, as well as his more underhanded, but necessary, dealings. Grant had personally seen to dozens of assassinations. He'd handled threats, or potential threats, to his power, personally, without ever letting Wilson know.

Grant knew how to clean up after himself. He knew how to use others. He knew how to recruit a man for one part of a job, and another man for another part, keeping them all in the dark about the whole project.

No one at the camp knew as much as Grant did. And he liked it that way. It was going to stay that way. It was partly how Grant kept an iron grip on the seat of power.

"Well?" shouted Grant, as neither nurse answered him.

The male nurse had entered the room. His arms and hands were shaking. Actually quivering.

"You were attacked, sir," said the male nurse.

The female nurse stood behind him, as if he'd protect her from Grant.

"Give me the facts. Don't prance around it. Spit it out." Grant was nearly shouting. He could feel the anger building up in his chest.

He glanced down again, noticing that he still had on his own clothes.

There was a chair in the corner, by the window. His holster and gun lay on the chair. It seemed that the rest of his gear, his knives, his compass, and everything, had been laid out neatly by his gun.

"Your personal secretary, Wilson, is missing," said the male nurse, speaking haltingly, apparently due to nerves. "The man guarding the stockade is dead. Gunshot wound. Name..."

"I don't need his name!" shouted Grant. "Give me the rest. Quickly!"

"We presume that Wilson, or his accomplice, attacked you. Perhaps they acted together."

"Accomplice?" said Grant.

The word triggered a memory. Something he'd forgotten.

There'd been someone.

A man named Max.

The memory came flooding back to Grant. The information he'd gotten from his informant. Information about a power struggle.

"So they're together? Have you caught them?"

"Not yet, sir. But we've dispatched Unit B. They're working on it as we speak, I'm sure."

Unit B was supposed to be the crack unit. The unit that did the special missions. The unit that was under Grant's personal control.

"Working on it? What the hell does that mean?"

"They're working on tracking Wilson and the escapee."

Grant didn't like the fact that Unit B had been dispatched without his own personal orders.

"Who dispatched Unit B? All their orders are supposed to be cleared by me, if not given explicitly by me."

"Saunders, sir. He installed himself in Wilson's place, after Wilson absconded."

Grant grunted his disapproval. He had never liked Saunders. He was a weakling. Someone who never stuck up for himself. He was just supposed to be there as a placeholder.

Grant had never expected that anything would actually happen to Wilson. After all, Wilson had hardly ever exposed himself to danger. He was an office man. A clipboard man. A paperwork man. A man who should have died from old age.

And Grant certainly had never expected that Wilson would betray him.

His blood was starting to boil at the thought of it. He felt the anger in his stomach. The hot anger was in his chest too.

His whole body felt energized. Hot. Angry. Ready for action.

Grant glanced down at the IV. He reached down and ripped it out of his arm.

"Sir!"

The male nurse was over at his bedside in a flash, grabbing the IV. Apparently he was about to attempt to put it back in Grant's arm.

"You're dehydrated, sir. You need to replenish your fluids," said the female nurse.

The male nurse was coming at him with the IV.

Grant felt the anger rising in him. He formed his right hand into a fist and backhanded the male nurse with a single, powerful blow. The male nurse reeled and staggered backwards, colliding with the wall.

The male nurse regained his balance and stood there, stunned, the IV still in his hand.

In a flash, Grant was up on his feet.

It felt good to be standing up. Standing was the position of commanders. Lying down was for suckers.

Grant's brain was working in flashes. Flashes of insight. Flashes of anger.

In a single stride, he reached the quivering male nurse who clung to the IV as if were a life raft.

Grant grabbed the man's neck with his left hand. His fingers tightened all the way around the neck. Squeezing.

Grant's right hand formed a fist and slammed into the man's face. Blood on the knuckles. Blood on the nurse's nose.

The nurse's head swung back, smashed into the wall. His eyes rolled back. Unseeing.

Grant released with his left hand. The male nurse, unconscious, slid down to the floor.

The female nurse shrieked.

Grant turned to her, his body big and menacing.

He felt as if he took up the whole room. That's how he felt when he was angry. Good and powerful. Full of possibility. As if the world was his. As he deserved everything he wanted. As if he was always right.

It was riotous anger. Good anger. Just anger.

"If you know what's good for you," growled Grant, "get me the following men..." And Grant named a half-dozen last names. They were the best of the best. The men who Grant had kept off Unit B so that he could use them when he really needed them, when something really crucial came up. They were men who'd proven themselves. Not just their skill. But their willingness to do whatever Grant asked. They were men who'd gladly put their lives on the line for him, no matter what.

And, most importantly, they were vicious. The kind of men who took pleasure in extreme violence. The kind of men who got a kick from killing, and an even bigger kick from killing in the most brutal way possible. Grant had personally seen all of the six kill. And all six, under Grant's supervision, had brutally tortured prisoners. Grant had watched them dismember a man, one limb at a time, until he was nothing but a torso and stumps for legs.

Grant and the six had chuckled as they'd watch the man bleed out onto the dirt.

Those had been good times. The kind of good times that not every man could appreciate. Wilson, for example, had to always be kept in the dark about such matters.

It had been several weeks since Grant and the six had had their fun.

Well, now was there chance.

The female nurse stood there, quaking in her slip-on shoes.

"Well?" shouted Grant.

She just gave a meek nod, turned on her heel, and scurried away.

Good.

She'd get the word out. She was too scared not to.

The six would be ready.

They'd be seven with Grant.

Normally they worked on their own and brought the hostages back to Grant so that he could watch the fun.

This time would be different.

They'd be surprised.

But Grant was coming with them.

This time it was personal.

This time he'd relish in the hunt itself.

He was going to find Wilson and deal with him personally.

No one betrayed Grant.

Not without consequences.

S adie woke up with a start

Somehow, despite the situation she'd fallen asleep. She should have been on high alert. She should have been watching for an opportunity. Watching for more danger.

But it was almost as if her body and mind had been on edge for so long that they'd just shut down.

She'd had strange dreams. Dreams that Max and her mother had come to rescue her. Max had a pump-action shotgun instead of his normal Glock, and he was ruthless with it, although he didn't actually shoot with it. Instead, he used it like a baseball bat, swinging it in long, high arcs. Her mother, instead of her normal rifle, was at Max's side with a pickaxe that she played like a guitar.

What did it all mean, that crazy dream? Nothing. That's what it meant. Not a thing.

It was just her mind making up a story. And for what purpose? She didn't know. She'd never gotten to that lesson in school, apparently.

Her own education had continued, of course, but not in the way that it would have had she remained in school.

How long had she been asleep?

She didn't know, but outside it looked like late afternoon. What had the sun been like when she'd arrived? She couldn't remember.

Sadie tried to move, the way she normally would upon waking, and she suddenly realized that she couldn't move.

She couldn't move her arms. Or her legs.

Not only that, but she couldn't feel them.

They were completely numb.

The realization of that sensation made her start to freak out. Her mind started racing a mile a minute.

Could she move her fingers? Her toes.

She tried. But she couldn't feel them.

Shit.

Her vision was still sort of blurry, the way it often was when she woke up.

She looked down, craning her neck.

She was in a weird position, like a crab on its back. Sure enough, her legs and arms were bound tightly together by rope.

The memories all came flooding back to Sadie.

Shit.

She'd shot Terry.

His wife had tied her up.

And then what?

Sadie looked around, craning her neck more. It was one of the only parts of her body that she could still move. And it was uncomfortable to do so.

It was a little back room. Some might have called it a mudroom. There was a small window there. There was some junk against the wall, and some more junk on a steel shelving unit, the kind that you'd typically find in a garage.

What would her mom have done if she were in this situation? What would Max have done?

Look for useful things. Find some way to influence the outcome, and do that to the best of their ability.

But Sadie couldn't move. Not really, anyway.

She *could* move her back, wiggling it as if she were a worm.

Maybe she could move this way. Maybe she could worm her way across the floor, find something to cut the rope with.

It was worth a try.

It was a horrible feeling, having her feet, legs, arms, and hands completely numb. Like everyone else, she'd experienced the sensation of pins and needles, and the progression of that, that lead to numbness.

But this was something different. This was complete numbness. She really couldn't feel them at all.

Would she ever feel them again? Or had the blood supply been cut off for so long that she'd never regain feeling or use of them?

It was a scary thought, but Sadie thought about what Max might do if he were in this situation. He wouldn't have wasted time worrying about a possible future without even figuring out how to escape.

He would have made escape his priority. He would have used everything at his disposal.

Sadie wormed her away over across the room. She made it about six inches. It was tough going. She was exhausted already. How did snakes move like this? It seemed to take a huge amount of energy.

The little mudroom that Sadie was in was small. Very

small. There was only about another two feet before she got to the steel shelving unit.

Sadie couldn't make out exactly what was on the shelving unit. Right now, it looked like some cans of paint. And something behind the cans. Maybe there were tools, or something that could cut the rope.

Sadie didn't have the slightest idea yet how she'd use a tool to cut the rope when she couldn't move her hands.

She'd figure that out when the time came.

The thing now was just to get there. Just get to that shelving unit.

It took her what felt like forever. Maybe in reality it was about a half an hour.

By the time she was just a couple inches from the shelving unit, Sadie was breathing very hard from exhaustion, and she felt even more exhausted than before. The feeling in her extremities hadn't come back. And now her back, for the first time in her young life, hurt her, and she understood what John was always complaining about.

Back pain sucked.

Just a couple more inches.

Sadie was going to do it.

She got herself ready for the last final push.

Then she did it, launching herself sideways towards the shelf.

She misjudged and launched herself too hard. She slammed into the metal shelves, her head knocking against a can of paint that was on the lowest shelf.

It hurt. But not that bad.

Her head flopped back, as if she was a rag doll.

Something on one of the upper shelves, that she couldn't see, fell off. She heard the things on the upper shelves knocking around as they destabilized.

A smallish can of paint hit Sadie in the neck and the jaw. It may have been a small can of paint, but it was still heavy.

There was pain. A good bit of it. More than she'd felt in a long time.

She didn't want to make any noise, but she let out a cry of pain.

The paint can hit the floor with a clatter. Sadie couldn't see it, with her head facing the other way, but she heard the lid pop off. The sound reminded her of a soda can being opened.

Sadie began feeling the paint. It was oozing around on the floor, the thick substance getting in her hair. It smelled horrible. She'd always hated the smell of paint, and it always seemed to give her a headache.

The door to the room flew open.

Sadie was already facing the door.

A woman appeared. The same woman Sadie had seen earlier. Terry's wife. What was her name again? Olivia?

Sadie scowled at Olivia. She was just as bad as Terry.

Suddenly, Sadie's expression changed from a scowl to one of fear. She couldn't help it.

She was afraid.

The woman towered above Sadie. She looked terrifying. There was a horrible look on her face. A look of disgust and despair.

What was she going to do?

Had Terry already died? Would he die?

"You'll be happy to know that my husband is on his last legs," she said. She spoke the words with disdain. She spoke the words with quiet, intense fury. "He's got minutes to live. Not hours."

Sadie decided to tell the truth. "I'm sorry," she said.

It was true. She hadn't wanted to shoot Terry. She'd

rather have had the situation turn out completely differently. But what other options had she had? She'd needed to try to defend herself.

"That's not going to do any good," said the woman, spitting on the floor, her eyes barely looking at Sadie, as if Sadie was some kind of disgusting specimen that was too horrible to actually look at.

It was clear what was happening.

Maybe this woman wouldn't have had kidnapped Sadie on her own. Maybe she had been a nice woman.

But her husband had done the deed. And now, with her husband dying from a bullet to the stomach, she was going to blame everything on Sadie.

Sadie was going to become the complete focal point for this woman's rage and despair.

"I'm still trying to decide what to do with you," said the woman. "Terry told me all about where you're from. Apparently you told him quite a bit on the walk here. So we know all about you."

"They'll give you whatever you want," said Sadie.

"We'll see about that," said the woman. "Terry thinks you're my ticket now. My ticket to survival. He says that your people will give me whatever I need. And now that he's going to be gone, I'm going to need all the help I can get. Terry may be be a shithead, but he's kept us alive. I can say that for him. He may be a coward and a jerk, but we're still alive. And I can't say it'd be the same without him. I'd have been dead a long time ago."

"They'll give you whatever you want," said Sadie, repeating herself. "But what's more, they'll take care of you. They're good people. We've taken people in before. Especially when they're eager to work and they're good people."

The woman raised her eyebrow skeptically.

The paint was really soaking into Sadie's hair. The smell was disgusting. Having that chemical smell so up close and personal made her want to vomit.

"They'll take you in," said Sadie. "If you bring them to me, they'll be so appreciative. My mom must be freaking out about where I am..."

"I'm not buying it," said the woman. "You may think I'm a fool, but I'm not. Even though I stayed with Terry... look where that got me. Alive, yeah, but stuck. Hiding all the time. It was hard for Terry to talk, but he managed to tell me everything you told him about your mom. She sounds like a fierce woman. Vengeful. Powerful. Strong."

"She is," said Sadie. "But she's also kind. And forgiving."

"Bullshit. I don't believe that for a second."

Sadie was shocked by the tone of the woman's voice. It sounded harsh. Very harsh.

"What are you going to do with me, then?" said Sadie.

"I haven't decided yet. Might be easier to get rid of the evidence. Terry's been wrong plenty of times before."

Get rid of the evidence?

Sadie knew what that meant.

"You can't kill me," she said. "I know you have a daughter my age. How would you feel if this happened to her?"

"That's what I'm trying to stop from happening."

"My mom would never do anything like that..."

"That's what you think now. But you're not an adult. When you're an adult, you'll understand. Sometimes you have to do terrible things. Even when you don't want to."

The woman was turning away from Sadie, and before her face fully turned, Sadie saw tears running slowly down her cheek. The tears caught the daylight in a strange way, seeming to sparkle.

Then the woman marched out, her footsteps heavy and hard. The door slammed behind her, and Sadie was left alone, with her head and jaw hurting, with her limbs hurting, with the horrible paint smell overwhelming her completely.

17

There wasn't time to explain it. Good thing John knew her well enough to know that there was a method to her madness. He knew that if she told him they were doing it one way, there was a very good reason for it.

Now, Georgia herself didn't know exactly what that reason was.

In fact, Georgia knew well enough, rationally, that shooting dead one of the men wouldn't do them any favors.

Better to just run for it before shooting. Even if she and John both got off good shots, there were still six men standing. And probably more in the truck.

She was going off a hunch. A gut feeling. Instinct that had come from months of this kind of stuff. Her brain had become good at analyzing and dealing with these kinds of situations, the way that a concert cellist might slowly develop an innate sense for when to play loud and when to play softly.

Her mind was evolving. Becoming the mind of a warrior.

Or at least someone who survived. Because, sometimes, staying to fight wasn't going to lead to survival.

Georgia knew she was right. She knew her gut feeling was right. And maybe it was good that John would believe her right away, without explanation, because if she'd explained it, maybe he wouldn't have wanted to risk his life based on a hunch.

It was a lot to ask of him.

But they were always asking a lot from one another.

He was already risking his life, trying to find Georgia's daughter.

Georgia readied her rifle. The scope was against her eye, pressed against her face. It felt good. Familiar. She knew what she was doing.

Her finger was on the trigger.

The man's head was in her scope.

Why were the men acting the way they were? It was strange behavior. Hadn't they spotted them?

Georgia couldn't worry about that now. She had to go with her gut on this one. There was too much information to process rationally.

Max would have had one approach. And Georgia had hers.

Neither was necessarily right.

The time was now.

Georgia squeezed the trigger.

The rifle kicked.

The man's head exploded inwards. His body sunk to the ground, falling rapidly.

Georgia's ears rang. She put the scope aside. Somehow, she knew it wasn't going to work for a second one. She knew it intuitively, just getting a sense of the men and who they were and how they moved.

Georgia knew that they'd be fast in responding.

She was already on her feet, the gun in one hand. Ready to run.

John was already off. Running. Several paces ahead of her.

Good. Just the way she wanted it.

A bullet slammed into a thin branch near her, the branch exploding on impact, shattering. A gun discharged, the sound echoing out.

Georgia was running. Sprinting. Following John through the trees.

She didn't turn around. She didn't listen for footsteps. She could barely hear anyway, over the roar in her ears.

John ran fast. Faster than she'd seen him run in a long, long time.

She managed to keep up with him.

Her breathing was heavy and ragged. She was sweating intensely. She felt the burn in her legs. She felt the pain in her knees. She felt the pain on the bottoms of her feet as her boots slammed into the earth.

She kept her arms pumping at her sides as best she could. The rifle slammed into her side, and into the back of her leg. Painful. Not too bad though. Nothing she couldn't deal with.

Finally, she couldn't take it anymore. She had to turn around. And she did.

There was no one there. She saw no one.

It made sense. If she'd been able to see them, she'd probably already be dead. That didn't make much sense. But in a way, it did. If they'd followed her closely, they'd have been in range to kill her. It wouldn't have been hard.

For some reason, the men had perhaps retreated. Or decided not to pursue. Maybe they were carrying something valuable in that truck. Maybe they were spooked, seeing one of their men die instantly like that.

Who knew? It didn't matter.

John hadn't turned around. He didn't know the deal. He was still running.

That was good. They shouldn't count their eggs before they hatched. They didn't want any false victories. Better to get a good distance away before resting.

Georgia saw it before she heard it.

John's head suddenly bobbed up and then down.

He let out a yelp. A noise of fear. A guttural sort of noise. An unintentional sort of noise.

He'd lost his balance or was in the process of losing his balance.

In another situation, it would have been almost funny. It looked as if he had suddenly decided to pull off a dance maneuver, as if he'd decided to bob his head like a chicken.

It looked like a stunt. Like a gag.

But it wasn't.

His boot must have gotten caught on something. Or his leg must have given out. Or he'd simply lost his balance for no reason at all.

Mere seconds later, he was flying through the air forward, as if he were taking an intentional dive into the dirt.

Georgia missed the next part. It all happened too fast. A tumble of limbs. A collision with the ground.

The next thing Georgia knew, John was on the ground. Face down.

He was grunting in pain.

Georgia stopped suddenly, threw her hands out to stabilize herself, so as not to run over John.

She looked down at him. Struggling to take in what she saw.

His right leg was clearly broken. The femur had snapped in two. The break allowed for an odd, impossible angle.

It shouldn't have looked like that.

Shit.

It was a bad break. A really bad one.

Georgia glanced behind her, turning her head. There was no one there. But that didn't mean they weren't coming.

Georgia ducked down, her hand moving carefully over John's leg.

The bone had broken through the skin.

It looked horrible.

Georgia had seen pictures before, but she'd never seen it in person. It looked worse than she could have imagined.

Blood and bone. Broken skin. Not a pretty sight.

John was, admirably, trying to keep his noises of intense pain to a minimum.

"Is it bad?" he managed to say, his voice barely audible over grunts of pain.

"It's bad, John."

"They're going to be coming. Leave me."

"You know I'm not doing that."

"You've got to. Think of Sadie. You're not going to find her if you're dead."

"Who says I'm going to be dead?"

"If you stay there with me, you're going to be," said John. "I don't want my last act to be to get you killed along with myself. This is my fault. My mistake. I'll take the consequences."

"What would Cynthia think of that? If I get back to camp and you're not there. I'll tell her that I left you to rot on the ground with a broken leg? I'll tell her that I didn't lift a finger to help you. And you think she'll be OK with all that?"

"We've talked about it. She'll understand."

"You've talked about it? I don't know what she told you, but let me tell you, there's no way she's going to be OK if you don't come back."

"She knows the risks of this lifestyle . We have an understanding."

"You may think you do. You may think you've accepted the consequences of being in a relationship. You may think that you're ready to lose her, and that she's prepared to lose you, but that's not the case. It's really not. So I'm not leaving you here. It doesn't matter what you say, so save your breath. We're getting out of here together, or we're not getting out of here at all."

"You... don't..." John spoke haltingly, grunting through the pain.

"Save your energy," said Georgia. "I'm going to get us out of here."

John just grunted. Georgia didn't know if he'd decided to listen to her and shut up, or if the pain had just gotten too great for him to talk.

Georgia's hands were on her rifle. She was looking around, putting her eye to the scope, taking it away. Trying to scout the whole area.

If the men were coming, they'd come soon.

If they came, the best-case scenario was that it was five men against one woman.

Georgia suddenly spotted John's rifle on the ground.

Crouching, she made her way over to it. Grabbed it from where it had fallen.

"Here," she whispered, stretching out her hand, holding the rifle so that John could grab it.

She didn't know if he'd be able to shoot.

He probably didn't either.

No point in talking about it much.

He'd shoot if he could.

And if he couldn't, then he wouldn't.

It seemed as if the only thing Georgia could hear was her heartbeat.

She stared into the distance, waiting for the men. Watching for them. Everything seemed to turn blurry as her thoughts turned towards her daughter.

Where was Sadie now? Would she ever find her?

The chances were slim that Sadie was alive. And even slimmer that Georgia would ever get to her, whether she was dead or alive.

Wilson was following Max along a back road. They were walking in the middle of it.

Wilson kept turning around. He was waiting for the moment when he'd see them all coming for them. He was waiting for the moment when he'd know that he'd soon be dead.

Of course, Wilson doubted they'd be killed on the spot. More likely, Grant would want to make an example out of them. Especially Wilson.

What had Wilson been thinking?

If he'd been smart, he would have let Max, the prisoner, die. He would have let Grant do what he'd wanted. Then Wilson could have snuck off into the night any time he'd wanted. He could have taken enough with him to carve out a comfortable little niche for himself somewhere far away, somewhere where no one would bother him.

But he hadn't. He hadn't done that.

He'd let his anger get the best of him. He'd let himself lose control.

And yet, despite losing control, he hadn't killed Grant.

Why?

It was as if Wilson had been unable to break completely free. Despite hearing what Grant had done, despite hearing how power-hungry and insane Grant had become, or had always been, Wilson had been unable to strike the final blow.

Not only that, but he'd prevented Max from doing so too.

He should have pulled the trigger himself.

He should have plunged a knife into Grant's heart.

At least that way, when Wilson drew his last breaths, he'd know that he'd done some good in the world. He'd known that the psychopath he'd served for too long was dead, hopefully rotting away in a shallow grave, his corpse indistinguishable from the millions of other corpses that littered the country.

"Max," called out Wilson, picking up his pace. It seemed as if Max was getting farther away from Wilson. He was moving an incredible pace. Limping along rapidly.

Max didn't answer. And he didn't turn around.

Wilson had given him one of his handguns, keeping the other for himself.

Wilson had the gun in his hand now.

The weight of it didn't feel comforting. It didn't reassure him.

The gun was a reminder of what was going to come. A fight. Violence. Death.

Wilson himself had devices and procedures for situations like this. He knew exactly what to expect.

He'd tried to tell it all to Max. Explain everything to him. But Max hadn't been interested. He'd just been interested in going. Getting far away.

But Wilson knew that getting far away didn't matter.

No matter how far they got, the militia men would

always be able to catch up to them. After all, they had fleets of working vehicles. Trucks. Cars. Motorcycles. Dirt bikes.

All working. All gassed up. All ready to hunt Wilson and Max down.

The alarms had been sounded early. Everyone had been on alert. Those on guard duty had responded, but hadn't left their posts, in case an attack was imminent. Those on reserve duty had responded, some of them filling out defensive positions, and others taking up the hunt early.

Max and Wilson had managed to evade the groups of the first responders.

And, so far, they'd been able to keep ahead of Unit B.

Unit B was a crack unit. A special unit. A unit of men who rarely had equals.

Unit B was scary enough. Terrifying, really. Wilson had seen the reports of what they'd done. They had no mercy. They were barely men. More like caged animals. In a fight, at least.

Unit B wouldn't be all. Grant would respond personally. With his own group. His secret group. The group that did the worst things. The unspeakable things.

Wilson shuddered. A chill ran down his spine. It wasn't a good feeling, being on Grant's bad side.

Why hadn't he killed him when he'd had the chance? Because he was weak. Horribly weak.

Wilson was suddenly overcome with shame. Horrible shame and self-loathing.

He couldn't do this. Who did he think he was? He was the man behind the desk. He didn't need this, dying out there, exhausted, dehydrated, starving, after days of being hunted like some animal.

Wilson couldn't do it. The emotions were overpowering. Simply too much.

He stopped in his tracks.

He stood for there a few moments, gazing off at Max's back as Max continued walking, getting farther away.

Max didn't notice. He didn't turn around.

Wilson felt so hopeless that he couldn't even tolerate the idea of standing up. It felt as if the whole world was pushing down on him, as it were all above him rather than below him.

He sank to his knees heavily. And then that seemed like too much effort to stay positioned like that, so he sank down, falling onto his side.

He lay like that, essentially in the fetal position, staring straight ahead.

Everything felt pointless. Everything felt impossible.

There was no answer.

There were too many problems.

"Hey!"

It was Max's voice.

Wilson ignored it. His hand relaxed its grip, and the handgun clattered to the pavement.

Footsteps nearby. Max's footsteps.

Wilson didn't move his head, but his eyes followed Max as he strode towards him with long strides.

"What the hell are you doing?"

Wilson said nothing.

Max extended a hand down, offering it to Wilson.

It was too much work to take it. Too much work to get back up. Too much work to fight it all.

Wilson ignored the hand.

Really, it was too much work to lie there. It was too hard. Maybe there was an easier way out.

"You know as well as I do that we've got to get going. Shit, you probably know it better than I do. They're coming for us, and they're not giving us any breaks. Like you said, they're not going to pull any punches."

"There's no point."

Max said nothing. Just stared at Wilson.

Wilson lowered his gaze, his eyes focused now on the pavement. The black. The yellow line. The way the pavement was chunky. It was all up close. All easier to focus on than what was really important, than what was really going on.

"I know exactly what they're going to do to us. There's no point in fighting back. I've never seen it work. I've been with Grant since the beginning. He's ruthless. You just don't even know. You think that..."

"I've met men like him before," said Max. "I know what they're about."

"I thought I knew him," said Wilson. "I thought he meant what he said."

"You can't trust what people say. Especially when they're talking about themselves. Everyone lies."

"I should have known that. Before the EMP, I was a... well, it doesn't matter now. What do you care what I was? But I knew people. I may have worked behind a desk, but I could still read people. I thought I knew the signs..."

"People are tough," said Max, his voice gruff and tired.

"I'm just going to end it all," said Wilson. He spoke quickly, and acted quickly as well. His hand seized the handgun that he had dropped.

Wilson felt as if he'd suddenly found the answer. He felt as if he'd been looking for this answer all his life, and as if his life had been nothing but struggle, toil and hardship.

It was if this is what he'd been looking for all along. But he didn't realize that his view of his life was distorted. It was almost as if they were false memories. He hadn't been like this before. Not all the time, anyway. He'd had his ups and downs through his professional life. Moments of depression. Moments of elation. All fairly normal. Fairly standard.

Wilson brought the gun around quickly, his arm swinging, his elbow digging into the pavement.

The muzzle of the handgun was pressed against his temple. He pushed harder, making the muzzle dig into his temple. Somehow the pressure felt good. Somehow the pressure felt right.

"You're going to have to do this alone," said Wilson. His voice sounded strange and far away, even to himself.

In a way, it was a shame to make Max do this all himself. To make him run and then get captured. To make him go through the torture and eventual death all by himself.

But really, what was the difference? It wasn't as if Wilson's presence was necessary. It wasn't as if Wilson's presence would alleviate Max's suffering

And even if it had, what did Wilson really owe Max? Max was a stranger. A nobody. Nothing more than just some guy.

Wilson has his finger on the trigger.

It was a strange sensation, knowing that he was about to pull the trigger. Knowing that he was about to put an end to it all.

It was such an easy answer. Such a brilliantly simple solution.

Why hadn't he thought of it before?

Were there any last thoughts? Anything he wanted to say before he did it? Before he did himself in?

No.

Nothing came to mind.

Before he could pull the trigger, something happened.

Something slammed into his wrist. Something hard. Pain flared through his arm.

Wilson yelped and dropped the handgun. His hand felt weak, with pain in it, and the dropping motion was automatic. Reflexive.

Wilson turned his head to look. To see what had happened.

It was Max's boot. Looking big. Imposing.

It was a horribly worn-out boot. Cracked leather patches. Frayed laces. Eyelets that were almost bursting out of the leather. The side of the sole cracked and shorn away.

The boot was pressed hard into the underside of Wilson's wrist.

"I can't let you go through with that," growled Max.

Something about his voice reminded Wilson of Grant. And he suddenly remembered that that had been his first impression of Max. That there'd been something Grant-like about him.

"It's the only way out for me," said Wilson, his voice weak and frantic.

Suddenly faced with the idea of not getting what he'd wanted, Wilson became desperate.

His heart started to pound. It felt like his eyes were bulging. Some tears started to flow. His body felt shaky, as if his blood sugar were getting low.

Wilson made a grab for the gun with his other hand. It was his only way out. The only thing he could think of.

Before he could grab the gun, Max kicked it. The gun went clattering across the pavement, bouncing slightly on the uneven road.

"It's the only thing I can do," said Wilson. "You don't understand what you're up against. You don't understand what we're facing."

Suddenly, Max's hands were on Wilson's shoulders. Max was leaning down over him, and now he pulled. Hard.

Wilson was pulled up roughly to his feet.

Max didn't look nearly as strong as he was. It was that wiry strength. That hidden strength.

Max pulled Wilson roughly towards him.

Max's face was right up against Wilson's. Wilson could see every feature, every pore. He could feel Max's hot breath.

It was like those army movies, where the drill sergeant got right in the face of the recruit. Yelled at him. Screamed at him. Threatened him, until he did what he wanted.

But Max didn't do that. he didn't yell. He didn't scream.

Instead, he spoke in a low, calm voice.

"We're not guaranteed to survive," he said. "But if you come with me, I promise that you have at least a chance. And you're right, you understand the consequences better than I do. You understand exactly what they'll do to us. That's partly what's making it so hard for you. It's easier if you can't imagine the consequences. It's easier if you can forget, if you can just plow on forward."

"Easy for you to say."

"Exactly," said Max. "I have a lot of practice with this. And because I'm good at this, I'm going to give you some tips. Tips on how to deal with this."

"It's not going to help."

"Even so, you're going to listen. Now the way I think about it is this: They're coming for us. They're people that we don't like. To put it mildly. Now do we want to make it easy for them? Do we want them to laugh about us later, when they're sitting around, cracking open beers that they scavenged from somewhere? Do we want to go out like that, or do we want to go down as legends, as people who fought for their survival, fought for what's right?"

"It doesn't matter," said Wilson. "After we're dead, we're dead. We just die, and that's it. Nothing matters after that."

Max shrugged. "Everyone has their own opinion on that," he said. "Me? I've got my opinions. I've got my beliefs. I keep them to myself. I'm not trying to convince you of anything. Except I need to correct you on one point. One crucial point."

"What's that?"

"You think that you're dead and that's that. It's not. If you die, the world's still here. Dying is the easy way out. The coward's choice and the hero's choice. Seems like a contradiction but it's not. If you die, Grant and the others are still there. Still able to terrorize. Still able to torture. Still as power hungry as ever. If you kill yourself, it's just selfish. Just the choice of a man who wants to close his eyes and pretend that the world will disappear when he does it."

Wilson didn't want to admit it to himself, but he could see that there was truth in Max's words.

Wilson felt something change in his body. It was his emotions. It was the tension that had been there, that had been holding his captive.

The tension was starting to melt away.

It seemed as if Max had provided him with the answer he'd needed. It was the way out that he hadn't been able to see before.

"If I'm already willing to die," said Wilson, his voice sounding strong and confident. He couldn't remember the last time his voice had sounded like this. "Then there's no reason to fear dying at the hands of those who follow us."

"Exactly," said Max. "Couldn't have said it any better myself."

Max released his grip on Wilson, and Wilson found himself standing up all by himself. Supporting his own weight. Standing on his own two feet. All the clichés applied.

He felt like a man.

It was a strange, sudden twist. A sudden change in outlook.

Suddenly, a plan started developing in Wilson's mind.

"OK," he said. "Here's what we've got to do..."

"What we've got to do is run," said Max. "They're going to be closing in. We didn't have much of a head start. Come on, I'm glad you're feeling better. But we've got to go."

"Run like rats in the night?" said Wilson.

"Exactly," said Max. "When the time comes, we'll fight. But for now, we run."

"I've got a better idea," said Wilson.

"You do?"

Wilson nodded. "I know how they work," he said. "I know what they're thinking. And, more importantly, I know what Grant is thinking."

"Then spit it out," said Max.

Max's posture said that he was ready to listen. That he was ready to change his plans.

The pressure was all on Wilson now.

But it felt good.

It felt good to be relied on. It felt good to want to fight.

Wilson was going take down Grant, even if it was the last thing he did.

He hadn't done it when he'd had the chance, and now he was going to make the chance. Create opportunity.

19

CYNTHIA

I
t had been a long, long night.

Mandy hadn't seemed to be getting better. In fact, it had seemed that with each howl, she was getting worse.

The pain had become intense. All sorts of pain. Seemingly diverse sources. Cramping. Sharp, shooting pain. Diffuse pain that seemed to be everywhere at once.

It was morning now. The sun was coming up.

Dan and James had been up all night on watch. They were serious about it. Serious about keeping everyone safe. Serious about defense and about duty. They'd learned well from Max.

Max had said that it'd been more important to impart an attitude on the kids rather than any specific skill. Of course, they'd been taught plenty of skills.

But if they knew that they could learn, if they understood what it actually meant to be able to learn, they'd be able to pick up the skill themselves when the time came.

"How's she doing?" said Dan, poking his head into the structure.

There was weariness on his face. Big dark bags under his eyes. But there was also determination in those very same eyes. Determination etched all over his face.

"She's OK. Thanks for the water. No word from Georgia or anyone else?"

Dan just shook his head, and ducked his head back outside.

It wasn't strange to see a kid acting like that. Not now.

He was as much of an adult as the rest of them. In a way.

In a way, he and James and Sadie had adapted better to the post-EMP world than the "adults" had. They'd known the pre-EMP world, but not for nearly as long as the others.

Cynthia, on the other hand, by comparison, had decades of the pre-EMP easy industrialized life. That was what she was used to.

In fact, it seemed as if Cynthia had had a harder time than the others adapting.

Sure, she knew about the chores she needed to do. She had learned them all. She had learned to shoot a gun. She had learned to fight. She had learned about knives and axes and about making fire. She'd learned about hunting and about foraging food.

But while the others always seemed to think about their plans for the future, about survival tactics, Cynthia's mind seemed to instead drift towards memories of her past life. Memories of life with her husband in their quiet little house. Memories of TV shows and good meals paired with good wines. Memories of nights out with friends at trendy bars, memories of walking down the dark streets of Philadelphia, swaying from happiness and drink, arm in arm with her husband.

Those days were all gone.

The others, sure, seemed to remember them. They seemed to suffer some brief momentary pangs of memory.

But with Cynthia it was different. She could tell it was stronger.

That was the way she was. She was more sensitive. She always had been.

She'd buried it all deep down. The others had no idea that she felt like this. They thought she was a no-nonsense woman. Practical. Didn't dwell in the past. Thought only of practicality and the future.

But that wasn't reality.

She was too sensitive for her own good. Back when the hordes had come, when Cynthia with the others had had to slaughter unending numbers of them, she had cried the nights away, weeping silently so that John wouldn't hear anything.

She still thought of those days. She still thought of the faces of the men and women that she'd killed. They were faces with the crazed eyes, with the wide pupils, with the gaunt intense lines of emaciation.

And now, just when everything seemed to be settling down, problems had started up again.

It was almost too much for Cynthia to deal with.

She hadn't wanted Max to leave. She hadn't wanted him to go off on his own. She didn't like the idea of him leaving Mandy here.

Sure, in a way it was a horrible thing for him to do. And in another way, it was noble. He'd do anything for a better world for his kid, even if it meant that he might never meet that very same kid.

The promise of a newborn in the camp had seemed... Well, it had buoyed Cynthia's spirits a little. It had made it seem like things would once again be possible, as if things wouldn't remain static and stuck forever.

Maybe they wouldn't have to live in hiding forever. Maybe eventually they'd burst forth back into the world.

The child had meant hope. It had been a symbol.

And now? That was all in jeopardy.

Cynthia had combed through the midwifery book by candlelight.

There were many things that could have been wrong with the pregnancy and the baby.

And Cynthia didn't have the power to do anything about them. Not one of them.

She had no training as a midwife, and the book didn't go into enough detail. It wasn't that sort of book.

And, anyway, when it came to serious pregnancy complications, the book pretty much just advised that the midwife take the pregnant woman to the hospital as soon as possible.

What good was that to Mandy and Cynthia? None.

So there was really nothing to do but try to help with the pain. Be there for her. Hold her hand.

Those kinds of things. Useless, really.

Cynthia preferred things that worked. Things like penicillin, which could arrest an infection before it got serious. The results were clear-cut.

She needed something like that now. But she knew that it wasn't going to happen.

Mandy's noises of pain had gotten so bad that Cynthia had figured that at best, Mandy was going to lose the baby.

At worst, they were going to lose both Mandy and the baby.

And Cynthia was going to have to watch it all happen.

Cynthia didn't know if she could bear to do it.

But who else was there?

She couldn't leave Mandy there on her own. That'd be cruel.

The kids couldn't handle it.

"How are you feeling?" said Cynthia, in her gentlest tones. She placed her hand lightly on Mandy's shoulder.

Mandy hadn't been asleep, but she'd been in some kind of dazed state.

She stirred a little now, moving her body somewhat restlessly, acting as if she had been asleep.

"Better," said Mandy, but her voice sounded weak.

But she wasn't grunting in pain. She wasn't panting laboriously.

"Everything feel all right?"

Mandy shrugged. "I guess so," she said.

"You seem like you're feeling a lot better actually. No more pain?"

"Not really," said Mandy. "I just feel exhausted. Depleted, I guess."

"Hmmm."

"Did you find anything that book? Anything that it might be?"

"A few things caught my attention, but..." Cynthia didn't quite know what to say. It was hard to find a delicate way to say that there was nothing they'd be able to do for any of those problems.

Mandy nodded, though, as if she already understood.

"I was worried about getting pregnant in the first place," she said. "It seemed crazy to want to bring up a child in this world."

"Life has to go on," said Cynthia. "Just because we don't have electricity, and the government had fallen away..."

"Yeah, that's what Max and I decided. Things have to

keep on going. You can't just pause life because..." Her voice sort of faded away.

It was one of those types of discussions, where they each started to say something that sounded like it would be dramatic and important, but then didn't quite know how to finish the sentence.

They sat in silence for a few minutes.

Mandy had her eyes fully open now. Her face looked like it had been through the wringer, with dried sweat, and, it seemed, even some new lines. Lines from dealing with the pain. Lines from the stress of the whole thing.

"Maybe I'm going to be OK," said Mandy, sounding as if she was nervous to even suggest the possibility. "I really don't feel that bad... Is there anything in the book about some condition that can come and go this suddenly?"

"Maybe. I'll have to look back through it..."

"Here, give it to me."

"You're feeling that much better?"

"Yeah. Good enough to read. Maybe not good enough to take a watch shift, or chop firewood."

"Here you go."

Cynthia handed the book to Mandy.

Mandy took it and began flipping through it.

"I guess we don't know if it'll stay gone, or if it'll come back. The pain, I mean. And the other symptoms."

"No," said Cynthia. "I guess we'll just have to wait and see."

And that was the truth. There wasn't anything they could do but wait and see.

Hopefully, Mandy and the baby would be all right.

Hopefully, nothing would happen.

How terrible would it be if Max returned, and there'd been some horrible problem with the pregnancy?

Or if Max didn't return at all? And his sacrifice had been completely in vain?

It all seemed too terrible, and Cynthia buried her face in her hands.

S adie needed to get out of there.

She didn't know how long she'd been lying there now, with the stench of the paint all around her, all over. She'd just been waiting for the woman to come back.

And when she came back, what then?

Would Sadie die? Would the woman decide it was easier to kill her?

Or would the woman have news of a ransom note that she'd somehow delivered to her mother?

Sadie couldn't see her mother taking the news well. But no doubt she'd come and rescue her.

But if her mother could have talked to her now, what would she have said?

She'd have told her to fight. She'd have told her not to rely on others for help. She'd have told Sadie to not count on anyone to come rescue her, not even her own mother.

She'd have told Sadie that it was up to her, and her alone. That she had to do it all herself. That she needed to be strong and courageous and clever.

But what was she supposed to do? She was tied up.

Completely. She couldn't move. She couldn't even feel her limbs.

What were the chances of different outcomes? What were the chances that Olivia would come back and kill Sadie?

Probably not great. How did she figure that? Well, it'd have to be based on revenge. And revenge only.

Why revenge only? Because she didn't seem like the kind of woman who had killed before. She had relied on her husband to do the dirty work for her. So even if she wasn't going to play the ransom game and try to use Sadie as a pawn in her survival game, she likely didn't have the courage to actually kill Sadie.

No, she wasn't the courageous type. Not like Sadie. Or her mother. Or Max.

Olivia was the type of woman who, if it served her purposes, would just let Sadie rot on her own. She'd let Sadie die of dehydration there in that stupid torturous little room.

Sadie wasn't going to let that happen.

She had to figure out something.

But what?

The situation seemed hopeless. She had nothing on her. She could barely move now.

She had no tools. Nothing to cut the rope with. No way to even move well enough if she did have a tool.

Sadie took a couple deep breaths. She was starting to panic. The situation was starting to seem even worse than hopeless. Her very thoughts were starting to feel completely pointless.

The breathing helped.

Helped keep her from panicking.

Panicking wasn't going to do her any good.

But neither was just lying there.

Her mind was racing. Trying to think of everything that Max and her mother had ever told her.

It was hard to remember everything. She'd told her a lot. They'd taught her a lot.

She remembered that Max had told her that even when it seemed like there were no options, when it seemed like there were no routes out, there was always something to fall back on. And that was the mind.

She couldn't remember when Max had told her that.

But he'd definitely told her that at some point.

Or had she imagined it? Had it just been some kind of cinematic dream?

Sadie didn't know.

But she knew that she still had her mind.

Sadie still had her mind.

Maybe she couldn't use her limbs. But she could use her mind. She could use her mouth.

Maybe she had a tool there in the house. Maybe it wasn't a traditional tool.

But she knew very well that there was a girl there her own age.

And Sadie knew how to talk to kids her own age. It had been a long time. But she could do it.

"Hello?" she called out, trying to keep her voice loud enough that it could be audible on the other side of the door, but not much beyond that.

Ideally, the daughter, Lilly, would hear the call, and not the mother.

Of course, Sadie really had no way to control that.

But she could hope.

And she could keep trying.

"Anyone there?" She called out again.

Nothing. No answer.

But Sadie did hear something. A noise on the other side of the door. Sort of like a scratching sound.

"I can hear you," said Sadie, going out on a limb.

She hoped that she was speaking to the daughter and not the mother.

One wrong move, the wrong thing said, and the mother might get pushed over the edge. She might wind up killing Sadie.

The noise stopped.

That meant they were listening. Whoever it was.

Sadie had to take a chance. This was her chance.

"I haven't seen anyone my age in forever," said Sadie. As she spoke, she realized how "adult" she sounded. Before the EMP, she'd spent most of her day with kids her own age in school. Now, she spent most of her time with adults, with the exception of her brother and Dan.

She had picked up the adult way of speaking, and she'd lost the slang phrases that had been so common to her speech before.

There was no response. But there was the noise of slight footsteps. A very faint sound.

"I know you're there," continued Sadie. "And I know you can hear me. And I know you're curious about me. Otherwise you wouldn't have been nearby. I know you're scared about what's going to happen to your dad. It'll be just you and your mom... it's a tough situation... I can understand. I've been there myself."

Sadie didn't quite know where she'd picked up this ability. But she recognized that it was something adults did, from time to time. It was manipulation, plain and simple. But sometimes it was necessary.

Still no response.

"Why don't you open the door?" said Sadie. "Aren't you curious about me? I know you've been here all alone with your parents. All cooped up... It's got to suck big time..."

Some of the slang was coming back, but it still sounded unnatural.

Sadie waited.

It didn't seem like anything was going to happen.

There was no noise.

And then it happened.

The door handle turned.

The door opened. Creaking on its hinges.

Sadie hoped it was the daughter, and not the mother.

She held her breath as the door continued to open.

She craned her neck.

High up above, where the mother's face would be, there was nothing. But below, there was a little girl's face.

She was about her own age. Maybe a year younger. Hard to say, because she was thin and small. It looked as if she hadn't been eating very much. More or less like the mother.

It was strange and sad to see that gaunt look on a child. Sadie realized that she'd had it lucky, in a way. She'd eaten much better than this child, for instance. Sadie had retained her strength, and even grown in height and strength since the EMP had hit.

Then again, what could be sadder than Sadie's current situation? It seemed likely that she'd die, so it didn't really matter if she was well fed or not.

The girl stepped into the doorway. She looked down at Sadie but didn't speak.

"Hey," said Sadie.

It was weird. Definitely weird. Sadie was speaking as if she were meeting a new potential friend on the playground at school. But in reality she was tied up on the floor.

"Hi. I'm Lilly."

"I'm Sadie."

"I know."

"How's your dad?"

"Not good. My mom's out there with him. She says he's going to die."

There were the remnants of tears on Lilly's face. But she seemed to be taking the imminent death of her father fairly well. Maybe she was in a state of shock?

"Don't you want to be with him?"

Sadie was being careful not to jump right to her situation, even though it should have been painfully obvious that something was greatly amiss with her. She couldn't move, after all.

"He told me to go away. He wasn't very nice about it. He wanted to spend his last... time with my mom." Lilly gulped as she spoke.

"That's got to feel bad. Is he always mean to you?"

"A lot of the time. Since the power went out, especially."

"That sucks," said Sadie.

Then Sadie waited. She said nothing more.

"What are you doing here?" said Lilly. "I haven't seen any other kids since... a long time..."

"Your dad kidnapped me," said Sadie. "You're not going to be believe me, but I heard about you and wanted to come see you.... I was just desperate to talk to someone my own age after so long... And then your dad decided to kidnap me and use me as ransom...."

Sadie didn't want to add, "so I shot him," even though it was obvious enough what had happened.

Did Lilly blame her for killing her dad?

Sadie was pretty sure that if the tables were turned, she'd be upset if her dad was dead.

But Sadie didn't know her dad. Not at all. So it was a little hard to imagine.

There was a long pause. Very long.

Finally, Sadie decided it was time. Time to make her offer. Time to risk everything.

"So," said Sadie. "Do you want to come with me?"

"Come with you?"

"Yeah. Back to my camp. You can live with me and my mom. My brother, too. And everyone else."

"I... can't leave my mom..."

"She can come too."

"I don't think she will."

"But what will you two do without your dad? Why don't you try to convince her to come?"

"She won't do it. She's too suspicious."

"Suspicious of what?"

"People. Other people. We almost got killed. The three of us. There were some... other people and they..."

"It's OK," said Sadie. "You don't have to tell me the story. But I wish you'd at least consider what I'm saying."

Lilly shook her head vigorously. "There's no way.... there's just no way..."

"What are you and your mom going to do then? If you don't use me as ransom, I mean?"

"We'll find a way, I guess. We don't really need that much to eat. My mom said we really only need 800 calories a day."

Before the EMP, Sadie wouldn't have known what 800 calories a day meant. Now, she had a very good understanding. She'd eaten 800 calories a day, and she'd been painfully aware of that fact all the while. It had been brutal. Her stomach had been in pain the whole time, and she'd been weak, with a horrible lack of energy.

"And that's for her..." continued Lilly. "I only need 500 'cause I'm just a kid. Not as much as an adult."

"But our metabolisms are faster," said Sadie. She didn't want to start any kind of argument, since that didn't really fit in well with her plan. But the words just tumbled out, like a reflex. "We burn more calories per pound of tissue. Our basal metabolic rates are much higher than adults."

"Oh," said Lilly. "I didn't know that. But I'm fine... 500 is enough for me... we'll get by..."

"I know it's going to be hard without your dad."

"He... wasn't..."

"What is it?"

"He wasn't... always nice to us... he's been getting meaner..."

"So it won't be that bad without him?" ventured Sadie. "Maybe it'll be a little better?"

Lilly made a non-committal sound and shrugged her shoulders. It was as if she couldn't actually admit the sad truth about her father.

"So," said Sadie. "Your mom's either going to use me for ransom... or what...? I don't think she's going to let me go.... your dad was telling her that..."

Lilly made a sound as if she was choking.

"You OK?"

It was weird. Sadie was the one tied up. She was the one in the bad situation. And yet she was asking Lilly if she was OK.

"Uh, yeah. I'm OK. I just get nervous sometimes... make that weird sound... sorry... they used to make fun of me at school..."

"Well, there's no school anymore," said Sadie. "That's really mean that those kids used to make fun of you..."

"The teachers too."

"That's horrible," said Sadie. "They shouldn't have done that."

"But they did."

"My friend, Max, he's always saying that the important thing is that we're alive now. The past is the past. And now it's the way past. The EMP destroyed our entire culture. We're living in a different world now. A different reality. A new reality...."

Sadie was aware that she didn't sound so much like a kid. She didn't sound like an adult either. She knew who she sounded like.

She sounded like Max. He'd been rubbing off on her. His vocabulary. His attitude. His take on life.

"I guess that's true," said Lilly. "I don't even know if..." She made that choking sound again but managed to continue. "The people I knew before... I don't even know if they're still alive... it's weird to think about... Like the people that I'd see at the grocery store when I'd go there with my mom... maybe they're all dead now... It's horrible... My mom and dad don't like to talk about it all... they like to pretend... but I think about it all..."

Sadie felt like she had connected with Lilly. At least somewhat.

It was time to go for it.

"Lilly," said Sadie. "If you don't want to come with me, that's fine. You and your mom are going to be all right. You've survived this long... But I need to get back to my family.... My mom's going to be worried about me... She's probably giving my brother hell for letting me get away..."

Sadie paused.

Lilly said nothing.

But Sadie could tell that Lilly was thinking. Thinking hard.

"Why don't you just untie me, Lilly? If the situation were reversed, I'd do the same for you... I really would... There's not much time... While your mom's busy, just cut the rope and I'll slip away. You won't have to tell her anything... You can just pretend you don't know anything, and your mom will just think I managed to get away on my own..."

Still no answer.

Just that strange choking sound.

"Come on, Lilly," said Sadie. "There's nothing to worry about. If you're going to do it, you've got to do it soon. I don't know when your mom's going to come back."

What Sadie didn't want to say was that she didn't know how much longer Lilly's father would stay alive. He might have already died, and Lilly's mother might be coming back soon.

And there was no telling what she'd do.

Sadie knew that people confronted death in various ways. And she knew that it was entirely possible that Terry's death would greatly upset Olivia.

It was very possible that Olivia would channel her sadness and hopelessness into rage.

And it was very possible that she would direct that rage at the person responsible for Terry's death.

If Sadie didn't escape soon, she might soon find Olivia standing over her in a rage.

Ready to kill her.

Sadie needed to get out of there.

21

GEORGIA

"You'd better leave me," grunted John. "Or I might just shoot you myself. If that's not an impetus for you to leave, I don't know what is."

"I don't believe you. Not for a second," muttered Georgia.

It wasn't as if she was putting a lot of thought into what John was saying. She knew he wasn't going to shoot her.

The five men were a much bigger threat.

They hadn't shown themselves yet.

But she knew they were there.

Unless they had retreated.

If, after a couple hours, they didn't attack, then maybe it'd be safe to try to head back to camp.

Georgia already knew what she'd do. She already had a plan. She'd make a rudimentary sled and throw John on it. She'd drag him back to camp. Then she'd head off again, looking for her daughter, provided she hadn't somehow returned to camp on her own.

Despite the intensity of her own situation, Georgia's mind was still fixed on Sadie. She was still thinking about her. She couldn't get her out of her mind.

That's just the way it was. That's how it was being a parent.

Georgia was starting to think that if Sadie was going to get out of whatever situation she was in, she was going to have to do it herself.

Georgia might not get out of her own troubles alive.

Hopefully Georgia had taught her daughter enough.

She'd certainly tried her best. She'd hardly ever done anything at camp without explaining to her children why she was doing it. She knew that, somehow, sooner or later, she'd no longer be around to teach them anything.

And they'd be on their own.

Maybe that day would be sooner rather than later.

Georgia had never thought she'd get to old age and die in her sleep. Well, she'd thought that before the EMP. And after everything had collapsed? No, not since then.

She'd figured she'd die fighting. Sure, there'd been times when she'd thought they'd all starve to death. Or worse.

But now it was pretty clear.

She'd go down fighting.

It wouldn't have bothered her, the fact of dying, had it not been for her kids.

Of course, she wasn't going to go down easy. The way she saw it, the more of these guys she took out, the easier it'd be on those who did survive. The easier it'd be on the good guys. On her kids. On Max. Should their paths ever cross.

Of course, maybe they wouldn't attack. After all, Georgia and John were no threat to them. They could just get back in their truck and continue on their way.

What did Georgia and John care about them? Let them do whatever the hell they wanted. They had some purpose with that truck, but it didn't interest Georgia.

Not one bit.

Georgia heard the gunshot before she saw anyone.

It was a tremendous crack that echoed through the area.

Georgia's ears rang.

Shards of wood exploded outward from a tree nearby. The bullet had missed. Struck the tree instead.

Georgia spotted the man a split second later.

She pushed her eye against her scope. Dialed it in.

She had him.

Right in the chest. No point going for anything fancy.

She needed this man down. Right away. Didn't matter so much if he died right away or not. She needed him incapacitated.

There was an old theory of war that said it was better to injure the enemy rather than kill them. That way, the other side spent more time and resources tending to their wounded than they did on fighting.

Of course, for that theory to be applicable, the enemy had to be civilized enough to care about their own wounded.

Georgia had a feeling that that sort of thinking had gone the way of the dodo since the EMP.

And she doubted that these five men cared whether or not one of their own went down. She didn't know why, but the way they moved, the way they acted, made her think that they were some type of mercenaries. Separate individuals connected only by the promise of some kind of payment.

Georgia took a shallow breath. Held it.

Her finger pulled on the trigger.

Her gun kicked.

The man fell.

"Spot me," hissed Georgia, to John.

"Got you," grunted John. The pain was evident in his voice.

She knew that John knew what she meant. She needed him to keep an eye out for anyone approaching. And for anything she would have missed with her eye glued to the scope.

This would save time. And time, in a fight like this, could mean their lives.

Georgia stayed as still as she could. She remembered seeing firefights in movies in which the characters would move around, twisting their bodies and doing all kinds of absurd movements as they dodged bullets.

Georgia knew that you couldn't dodge bullets, no matter how badly you wanted to.

The way she was going to have the best chance of surviving was by shooting the enemy as fast as she could.

They were showing themselves now, emerging from out of sight.

She didn't bother counting them. She needed to kill them, not count them.

She had another one in her sights.

She ignored the bullets burring themselves into the dirt around her. She ignored the bits of dirt and the small rocks that rained against her legs. She ignored the sounds of the guns cracking as they fired.

She ignored the shouts of the men that she couldn't hear.

She only listened for John's voice.

And she didn't hear it.

She had to trust him. She had to trust that he'd alert her to someone approaching up close.

If she didn't trust him, she'd lost time. Valuable time. Making her more likely to die.

Georgia pulled the trigger.

Her gun kicked.

The man didn't fall. Blood appeared on his arm. His mouth opened in a scream.

She'd missed. Not completely. But she hadn't made him fall.

But maybe she'd disabled him.

She doubted he'd be able to shoot her.

More cracks of guns.

Georgia ducked her head down.

The earth around her jumped up as bullets struck it.

So far, she wasn't hit. She didn't know how.

Apparently John wasn't either. Unless he hadn't made a sound.

Georgia was about to go up for another shot when she was hit.

It was her leg.

She felt the pain. A burst of intense pain that didn't dissipate.

She knew the feeling well. After all, she'd been shot before.

She didn't yelp in pain. She didn't cry out. It was easier to do since she knew the whole routine from before. She'd been through it all before. She remembered the sensation of pain well.

Georgia didn't want the enemy to know that she'd been shot. It would only embolden them. It would only make them fear her less.

She knew that she needed to be an impossible enemy. An all-powerful, skilled enemy. Even if these men didn't admit it to themselves, they feared her. And that meant she was more likely to survive.

But really, how good were her chances?

By her count, there were three men left.

She didn't see them out there. Where had they disappeared to?

What would happen? Would a single bullet suddenly strike her, piercing her skull, shutting her consciousness off instantly?

That wouldn't be a bad way to go.

Statistically, though, it wasn't likely.

What was more likely was that she'd keep receiving bullets. Her body would shut down system by system.

She'd get struck, for instance, in her arm. Then she'd lose its function. And she'd become more likely to get hit again.

Right now, though, no one was shooting.

No one seemed to be out there.

Had they retreated?

"John?" said Georgia. "You still with me?"

"I'm here," said John.

"You see anyone?"

"Nope."

"You holding up?"

"More or less. You?"

"I got shot. The leg."

"Is it bad?"

"Not too bad. Not too good."

They weren't speaking loudly. They didn't want to cover up any noises of an approaching enemy.

It was easy to hear the intense pain in John's voice. And it was obvious that he was trying to not let it show.

Georgia could hear the pain in her own voice. And she knew that John could too.

It was a strange conversation.

There was that feeling that this might be their last

conversation. But it didn't feel like it did in the movies, when the slow-motion effects came on, and intense music gave the scene a timeless feeling.

No, there wasn't any special feeling. Just regular old pain. Just regular old fear. Just slightly fumbling hands, shaking from the adrenaline. Just the thoughts of how to survive.

"What are they going to try?" said John.

"You don't think they've retreated?"

"No," said John. "They may be acting weird. As if their under orders. But they don't seem like they're going to retreat."

"I think you're right," said Georgia, pausing to make sure she didn't miss any sounds around them. Like the sounds of footsteps.

"So how will they come at us?"

"I think they'll send one guy to get close to us," said Georgia. "And keep two in the back, distracting us."

"I'm keeping my eyes..."

A gunshot interrupted John's thoughts.

The gunshot was loud. A loud crack.

Georgia felt the bullet. It felt like it scraped across her thigh. Or maybe it buried itself inside it. Hard to tell without looking.

Georgia had the scope to her face.

She had the man in her sights.

Same deal as before. She pulled the trigger.

It was a good shot. She hit him.

Right in the neck.

A spot of blood appeared there as he fell to the ground, his arms spasming, his weapon dropping away from him.

There was no time to celebrate. John let out a scream.

A loud scream.

The crack of a gunshot. Right beside her. Very close.

No time to worry about who'd shot who.

Georgia flipped herself around as quickly as she could. She didn't think her leg would support her weight. But she needed to at least face the attackers.

She saw them.

Two of them. Standing there. Guns in hand.

John was there. Still breathing.

Whoever had shot had missed.

Georgia's mind was racing. The moment seemed stuck in time, as if time was moving in slow motion.

But it still wasn't like the movies.

Everything had an empty, hollow sort of quality to it. Her movements felt fast. Her body felt light.

Georgia had been right and wrong about the enemy's plan. They'd tried to distract them, while also going in for an up-close attack. But they'd left one man behind in the distance.

They'd left that man there as a suicide sniper. A man who wasn't going to make it.

The two who'd come in up close thought that they were the ones who were going to make it.

Not if Georgia could help it.

Time still seemed to be moving slowly.

John was bringing his rifle around. Lying on his back, he swung it down from over his head. He got it leveled at one of the men. Not bothering to really aim it, he shot it like he was a cop in the 1950s, shooting a revolver from the hip.

The man's chest exploded. Inwards and outwards at the same time. A splatter of gore. Blood, bone, and heart tissue.

His body seemed to remain standing in the deafening noise of John's gun.

One man left.

Georgia was about to do the same with her rifle. She was bringing it around.

But before she could, the man threw himself on top of her.

He did it as if he were a track and field athlete, making a crazy jump forward across the finish line, trying desperately to win the race, to break the record, to attain glory for himself despite the imminent threat of physical harm.

Georgia grunted as he fell on top of her.

He was heavy. The sharp parts of his body dug into her flesh. Sharp pain.

The impact of his heavy body knocked the breath right out of her.

She dropped her own gun. Simply let it go. It wasn't going to do her any good. It was too long.

Georgia didn't know where his gun had gone. Had he dropped it as he'd jumped on her?

His hands and arms were moving around. He was trying to get them into position.

Georgia's hands were pinned down underneath him, against her belly.

Her leg was still throbbing and shooting pain. It made her feel weaker.

But even if she'd had her own strength, she didn't know if it would have been enough.

Georgia tried bringing her knee up, to hit him in the crotch, but he blocked it, tightening his legs together.

With a flourish, he suddenly brought his hands up and out.

The next thing he did was wrap them around her neck.

They were strong hands. Wiry. Long fingers.

He had a good grip.

She used the only weapon she had left. Her teeth.

She lunged forward, chomping down on his neck as hard as she could.

He yelled in pain. A high-pitched wail.

But he didn't release her.

"John!" screamed Georgia. "Do something!"

She could barely get the words out. And when they came out, they sounded garbled. She didn't feel like she had much time left.

There wasn't much air in her lungs.

She was already out of breath. Already feeling like she was suffocating.

The hands weren't tightening around her neck, because they were already as tight as they could get.

She tried to speak more. She tried to shout. She tried to cry for help.

But no sound came out.

Where was John?

She could hear something. Some kind of scuffle. Some muffled shouts. She couldn't see what was happening.

As so often had happened in Georgia's life for one reason or another, it was up to her again.

If she was going to survive, she was going to have to make it happen. And it didn't matter whether she had pain or whether she was weak.

She'd either find a way to live.

Or she'd die.

She probably had mere seconds left.

Her vision was funny. Black around the edges.

Strange flashes of light in her field of vision, as if she was staring down the end of a flashlight.

The pain in her leg had gone. Vanished. Her body was focusing only on the absolute essentials. With mere seconds left to live, what did it matter if her leg hurt or not?

There wasn't much point in her leg sending those pain signals.

She didn't know what she did.

Later, she couldn't remember.

She couldn't distinguish between the different parts of her body.

It was as if everything simply acted together. In complete unison.

She threw herself forward.

All her strength. All her power.

She knocked into him.

Hard.

The hands released themselves.

Georgia's hands were going wild. Looking for something.

For some weapon.

Her knife was on her belt. She went for it.

But something was in the way.

She was gasping for breath. Still felt like she was unable to breathe.

But she couldn't let that stop her from killing this man.

He needed to die.

Fast.

It was an animalistic struggle.

She barely knew where she was or where he was.

Their bodies were still twined together. Mostly on their sides. Moving constantly. A constant struggle. Impossible to tell exactly what was what, or where it all was.

Her hand found something. Something hard.

Probably a rock. Hopefully a rock

Georgia didn't waste time wondering about it. She swung.

Swung hard.

It smashed into his skull.

Blood everywhere. The bone caved in, like pieces of shattered peanut brittle.

Brains oozing.

His body went limp, fell away from hers.

Georgia's eyes darted over to John. Now she could see him, without the body in the way.

There was another man.

Had she miscounted? Had they sent someone else?

The two figures were barely distinguishable. It looked more like a single animal creature that was fighting itself, tearing itself apart, biting itself.

The one part of the "creature" that Georgia could really identify as belonging definitely to John was his broken, busted leg that stuck way out, the bone clearly visible.

He must have been in so much pain.

But it didn't stop him from fighting.

They were biting each other. Deep bites that drew blood and tore flesh. Not the sort of bites that kids used when they were mad. No, these were animal bites, the type that a wild animal would use when fighting for its life. Human teeth may not have been primarily a weapon, but they worked pretty well. They could do some damage.

Georgia had her options. Her rifle. Her hands. Her knife. The rock.

Each had advantages and disadvantages.

She managed to stand up. Walk forward a little, slowly, limping.

Her leg was going to be a problem on the way back to camp. Better worry about that later. For now, she could manage to stand up. She could grit her teeth through the pain.

If she used the gun, she might kill John.

If she used her knife, she also might kill John. But the chances were lower.

No reason to think about it too much.

Her hand went to her knife. Fingers wrapped around the handle.

She threw herself forward, down onto the man, striking with her knife at the same time, plunging it into the middle of his back.

He let out a noise. A squeak. A squeal of pain.

John grunted.

Georgia's leg flared with pain and gave out. She tumbled down, falling too heavily to the ground.

22

MAX

Max's leg was killing him.

He and Wilson were both covered in sweat. They'd been walking, or hiking, at a fast pace for the better part of five hours.

They knew that they were being followed.

They knew that the enemy wasn't that far behind.

Occasionally, a gunshot would echo through the area. Occasionally, a bullet would lodge itself int he ground near them.

But neither had been hit. Not yet.

"How far away are they?" said Max, breathless, panting as he spoke.

His hand was sweaty, and he had to make sure to keep a good grip on his gun as he walked.

Wilson was walking a little bit behind Max. They had been switching positions, and eventually Max had over-taken him.

It wasn't that Max wanted to expose Wilson to more danger. But it was that without Max pushing them to go faster and faster, Wilson would have lagged behind.

"Half a mile, maybe," said Wilson. He sounded more out of breath than Max. Much more out of breath.

"You still think it's Grant himself?"

"No doubt."

"With the others?"

"The crack squad, yeah."

"So the first group... they're..."

"...off in some other direction, most likely."

"So how many are we dealing with?"

"Four. Maybe. There are more, but they're not with him... off in another direction... maybe trying to cut us off... we need to watch for that..."

"Including Grant."

"Probably."

"How do you know it's Grant himself?"

"I heard him. His voice... unmistakable... Shouting orders..."

Max didn't know what to do.

Sure, he had been in plenty of bad situations. Since the EMP, it had seemed like his life had been one constant appraisal of serious danger, one endless stream of life-or-death decisions.

But never before had Max felt like he really didn't know what to do.

There'd always been a set of options. There'd often been tough decisions. Tough choices. Hard calls.

He'd had to rack his brains plenty of times before. He'd had to go with his gut. He'd had to run scenarios through his head. He'd had to just go with his instinct.

It had always more or less worked out.

But now?

Max didn't think it was going to work out.

What were they going to do?

Sooner or later, they'd tire.

And soon enough, Grant's men would overcome them.

According to Wilson, Grant and his men had access to ample quantities of not just traditional pharmaceutical-grade amphetamine, but other substances as well. Things like modafinil, that were used by Air Force pilots during military exercises. They were the updates, improved amphetamines, that could keep men going for days and days without fatigue.

It wasn't going to end well.

Max and Wilson weren't going to be able to outrun them. They weren't going to be able to hide.

They were going to have to fight. There were no two ways about it.

Max stopped suddenly in his tracks.

Wilson almost ran into him, coming up from behind.

"What are you doing?" said Wilson. "Come on. We've got to keep going. They're getting close."

Wilson turned and looked back anxiously.

"This is it," said Max. "Come on. Get ready. This is as good a place as any."

"Are we going to die?"

"Most likely," said Max.

Wilson's face showed his terror. But it seemed that he was able to pull himself together.

Max readied himself, getting down on the ground, gun in front of him.

Ready to shoot. Ready to die.

Wilson did the same. Slightly off to the side.

There were some obstacles, some trees that provided some cover. But not much.

There wasn't much point in trying to hide themselves, or trying to delay the inevitable.

Grant and his men would come up, and there'd be a gun fight. If Max and Wilson hid themselves, then they wouldn't be able to shoot.

"Better to just get it over with," grunted Max.

"What?"

"Nothing," said Max, speaking no more.

His leg hurt. His whole body hurt. He thought of Mandy and hoped she was OK.

Max's hands were right on his gun. Gripped hard. Not too hard.

His palms were sweaty. His whole body was sweaty and uncomfortable. Somewhat itchy, too, strangely.

But what did he expect? For death to come on in a nice, pleasant way? Did he expect to die while feeling great, while on top of the world?

No. He never had. He'd imagined this moment countless times before. He'd known it would come. He hadn't known when. But he'd known that it would be like this. He'd known that it'd be painful and unpleasant.

What were the chances he'd die immediately? Not good.

If Max understood anything about Grant, it was that he was power hungry. And probably a sadist. Willing to do anything to stay on top. A sick man.

Grant, if he could, would have Max tortured.

It would happen fast. Max would get hit. A bullet here or there. Lodged in a leg or abdomen. Not enough to kill him. Just enough to incapacitate him.

Then he'd be taken by Grant and his men. Maybe tied up. Maybe just beaten until he was further incapacitated.

Then the imaginative things would start happening. From what Max had heard from Wilson and from the people in the stockade, the knives would come out.

Max would get carved up like a Christmas turkey.

He wouldn't enjoy it.

Maybe they'd be the worst moments of his life. Maybe not. He didn't know.

Max wasn't scared of torture.

He was scared of dying. That was normal. He couldn't help it. No point in fighting it.

The dying would end the torture. It would last a few minutes. Maybe a few hours or days if he was really unlucky. And then it would be all over. And after that, what difference would it make to anyone? What difference would it make to Max that he'd spent his last moments in intense physical and mental pain? None. He'd be dead.

Max saw it happen in a flash.

The men came rushing up. Four of them.

Grant was in the rear. Massive. Bigger and more powerful looking than the other men.

Grant's little unit wasn't expecting to find Max and Wilson there. They were expecting to find empty ground. They were expecting to keep chasing Max and Wilson.

So they weren't ready to fight. Not yet.

Max, though, was ready.

His trigger finger was moving. It seemed almost automatic. Almost as if he wasn't even thinking about it.

His gun kicked. No one fell. Someone was hit, but they kept going. Maybe a result of the drugs. Who knew?

Max wasn't expecting what happened next.

It all was happening so fast.

Someone was rushing towards the oncoming men, and for a moment, Max's brain couldn't comprehend who or what it was.

Then he realized that it was Wilson.

Wilson, rushing the oncoming men as if he were... well,

there really was no comparison. Max didn't know what it was like. It was like nothing he'd ever seen.

Wilson held his gun at his hip, running as fast as he could, faster than Max had ever seen him run during their escape.

It was like Wilson was a crazed warrior, carrying a flaming spear.

"Aghhhh!" screamed Wilson, at the top of his lungs. More shouted words came out, but nothing was intelligible. The only thing he communicated was that he was in a rage, that he was attacking, that he was using everything he had.

This wasn't just a last-ditch effort. It was something more.

Wilson had decided how he wanted to go out, how he'd wanted to be remembered.

Wilson went down in a flash.

Guns fired. Gunshots echoed.

Wilson was on his way down.

But not without firing shots of his own.

His gun went off like a cannon.

Pretty close range too.

Since, no matter how fast Grant's men reacted, it wasn't fast enough. Wilson had managed to get close to them. He'd managed to do the impossible, to give Max and him a tactical advantage when one hadn't been there to begin with.

Wilson got two of them. Hit them in the stomach. Which was pretty good, considering he wasn't really aiming at all. He was just firing from the hip, like he was in some old cowboy movie.

Then Wilson was down on the ground.

Max had fired three shots of his own.

It would have been miraculous, had Wilson not died in the process.

Max's ears were ringing horribly. His heart was pounding.

When it was all over, mere seconds later, there was only one man still standing.

And it was Grant.

Tall and massive Grant.

Fury on his face. A mean face. A horrible face.

Max took aim. He tried to take his time, while moving swiftly. His hands were steady.

Max knew he could make the shot.

Grant wasn't fast enough. In fact, Grant didn't seem to be acting rationally. He had dropped his gun. A long gun. Dropped it to the ground.

Grant's face was twisting, transforming. His mouth was open as he was screaming.

Max couldn't hear Grant's screaming over the intense ringing in his ears.

Max didn't know what he was saying.

But he saw what was happening.

Grant's desires had shaped his behavior. They had overtaken him. They had prevented him from thinking or acting rationally.

What Grant should have done is stood in place and shot Max to death.

But he didn't.

Now the ball was in Max's court. All he had to do was shoot.

He pulled the trigger.

Nothing.

No kickback.

No noise.

The gun was jammed. Just an empty trigger pull, accomplishing nothing.

Grant was coming at him fast. He looked like a linebacker. A linebacker who could do the 100 in 10 seconds flat. A linebacker who knew how to sprint, who knew how to pick up his knees, who knew how to move his arms. He knew how to propel himself forward.

He was mere feet from Max when he launched himself forward. Half-jump, half just thrusting himself froward

Max had no knife. No working gun.

Wilson's gun was far away.

This was going to be hand-to-hand combat. This was going to be a fight to the death. Nothing but their hands.

Unless Grant pulled a knife.

Anything was possible.

Grant's huge body smashed into Max.

It was hard to tell what was happening.

The impact seemed to make Max's vision go blurry for a moment.

And it stayed blurry.

Grant's hands were huge. Abnormally large. And strong.

His hands were around Max's neck. Grant's legs were splayed out as he crouched over Max's body.

Max was on his belly. Grant's breath was hot and close to his neck.

"You're going to die," hissed Grant, his voice deep and intense. "But don't worry, it's not going to happen fast... I'm just going to choke you out... when you wake up you're going to be in more pain than you've ever imagined..."

So Max had been right. Grant wanted to prolong his suffering.

Not that it mattered much.

"You hate me more than Wilson?" Max managed to say, despite the hands around his neck.

"Wilson..." grunted Grant, not adding any more.

"He's still alive," said Max.

It was a classic trick. The classic trick. It was a variation on "look, what's that over there?"

But it worked. Even if it was dumb, it still worked.

Grant looked, turning his big massive head on his big muscular neck.

Max brought both his legs up at the same time, as hard as he could. He had to pull them backwards, since he was on his belly.

It was his knees that connected with Grant's groin.

Max kicked backward with everything he had.

And it made a difference.

Grant squealed in pain. A high-pitched squeal.

Max didn't know how he did it but he managed to squirm his way out from under Grant, breaking free of the hands on his neck that were weakening.

It was all a blur.

Hard to say what happened in what order.

But now they were locked together, like wrestlers. Both of them on their knees. Both of their heads pressed against each other. Max's forehead hurt from the pressure.

Max's neck hurt from the strain of pressing as hard as he could against Grant's.

Grant's face was red. His cheeks were puffed out. His teeth were gritted. He wore an intense grimace.

"You're going to wish you were dead," hissed Grant.

Max didn't waste his breath talking. He didn't waste his energy.

But he knew what to do. He had to trick him. Distract him.

Max smiled. A big, creepy smile. Showed all his teeth. Really got the corners of his mouth up high.

It unnerved Grant. Max could tell that much.

It gave Grant just that moment of hesitation that Max needed.

Max had spotted the knife on Grant's belt earlier.

He reached for it now, completely blind, his eyes staying locked on Grant's, his forehead staying pressed hard against Grant's.

Grant's hands were once again at Max's throat, but it didn't matter. Max ignored it and just kept on flashing his absurd smile, as if everything was fine with the world or it just really didn't matter, as if he'd just completely lost his mind.

Max moved fast. Trying to get the knife.

It was hard doing it blind.

Max's first attempt missed. Instead, he just grabbed a bit of Grant's thigh.

It was as if he were making an awkward pass at him or something.

Max's hand fumbled around.

Found the knife.

It was a fancy fixed blade in a fancy holster.

The sheath was leather. Fortunately, there was no small piece of leather that snapped in place, securing the knife.

The knife stayed in just by friction. The sheath was tight.

Max wrapped his fingers around the cool handle. It was a strange-feeling material. Without seeing it, he knew it was something fancy. Something strange. Maybe some kind of rare stone. Pearl? Was that possible?

It didn't matter.

Max had been ignoring the hands around his neck. But

now he couldn't ignore the light-headed feeling, the sensation that he was about to pass out from lack of oxygen.

He had mere seconds.

Max pulled the knife from its sheath. He moved fast.

He moved his hand to the right, swinging the knife out far. Then he brought it back, moving as swiftly and as forcefully as he could.

The blade of the knife plunged into Grant's side.

Grant let out a grunt of pain, but managed to keep his eyes focused on Max's, and his fingers around Max's throat.

Max had never felt this lightheaded. Never felt so close to passing out.

It was almost like he was drowning. There was some distant memory from somewhere that was trying to surface, but it stayed put.

Max brought the knife back out. Then in again, plunging it into Grant's body.

Grant was a hardened, muscular man. But it didn't matter. The knife was sharp. It was double-edged. It was a real weapon, with a sharp point. And it plunged through Grant's muscles easily, slicing them apart as if it were surgeon's scalpel

The hands around Max's neck were loosening a little.

"You'll never..." growled Grant, bits of his spittle flying and hitting Max's face.

Grant's eyes had fury in them. They were locked onto Max's.

Max stabbed him again. And again.

And again.

By the time he'd stabbed him for the tenth time, Grant was done.

His eyes were blank. Pupils rolled back in his head. A

strange frothy substance on the corners of his lips. His hands had gone limp.

Max kept the knife in, driving it in even harder.

It took a huge effort to push Grant's inert body off of him.

But he did it. Grunting in pain and exhaustion.

There was blood soaking the hand that he'd stabbed with. Blood up to nearly his elbow. His hand felt cold and weak from the intense effort.

Max's neck hurt.

It seemed like he couldn't quite get enough air to breathe.

He staggered away from the scene, his eyes casting around on the ground.

He didn't know if everyone was dead yet. He needed a weapon. There was no time to celebrate.

He found it. A handgun someone had dropped. Not his own Glock, but it would have to do.

Grant was dead. His body was still. Max walked back over, checked the pulse.

No pulse.

Good.

Max made the rounds.

Wilson was obviously dead. Shot to pieces. His body was torn up from the bullets. A gruesome sight. No point in even checking the pulse.

The three others were on the ground. Max went to them each in turn.

The first two were dead. No pulse. Stone-cold dead. Good. Easier that way.

The third was still alive.

Max didn't have to take his pulse to find that out. When

he got close, he could hear the man's ragged breathing even over the roaring in his ears.

The man was spread out, stretched out. Lying face-up on his back. His arms were out to his side, spread all the way out.

The man had a short haircut. Reminiscent of the military.

He had a well-developed musculature. Impressive in these lean times when food was scarce.

Max didn't give his action a second thought. He pressed the muzzle of his gun against the forehead. Squeezed the trigger.

Point blank. Messy. But he didn't have time to try to play nice and clean.

Another life lost. Another human dead. Out of how many?

Max didn't know. But he wasn't going to be another statistic.

Now that he'd somehow defeated the undefeatable crack team, he knew he could get back to the camp alive. He knew he could outpace the other teams that were farther off course, father behind. Maybe they wouldn't even pursue him.

It was all because of Wilson. Wilson's sacrifice.

Max glanced down at Wilson's destroyed body. He owed his life to this man.

But Max didn't let his gaze linger long. He didn't let himself get too sentimental. Instead, he started digging through the pockets of every man there. And that included Wilson.

Max took would be useful to him. It didn't take long.

He'd lost his own gun. His Glock. But he'd gained others.

It wasn't the actual gun so much that mattered, but what

you did with it. And things like knowledge and circum-stance. And luck. Luck had a lot to do with it.

Less than ten minutes later, Max was leaving the bodies behind.

He had a pack full of the gear he'd harvested. He had guns and he had ammunition. He had food and he had water.

Most importantly, he knew where he was going.

His neck hurt and his body was tired. His leg hurt, as it almost always did.

Max set off at a good pace, not wanting to waste any time.

He didn't glance back. Not once. He didn't need to the see the bodies again. They were just dead people. Nothing useful left there.

Someone would find them at some point. Maybe other members of the cult-like militia camp that Grant had run.

Max would make it back to his own camp, an entirely different sort of camp.

He'd travel mostly at night. He'd take his time, doing everything safely. He'd make sure he got back. He'd make sure that he was there for Mandy when their kid was born.

Max was tired. Exhausted. But it didn't matter. He'd been through this sort of thing before. He knew that his body wouldn't give out on him for several hours more. He knew that although he'd already pushed himself, he could keep pushing himself.

Max understood the limits of his body. He understood what it could take.

He knew he'd live.

It was a little strange, heading back from the camp.

He'd left his own wife to try to make a difference. He'd

thought, on setting out, that he was too hardened and jaded to be caught in the idealism trap.

But he'd been caught in it nonetheless. He'd thought that he could make a difference. He'd thought that he could change the world.

When, in reality, all he could do was keep himself, his family, and his friends alive. Anything more than that was a pipe dream. And he needed to realize that if he wanted to stay alive.

This tangent with Grant had been nothing more than a dangerous delusion.

But had it been a waste of time?

Max didn't think so.

After all, the demagogue was dead. The man that Max had heard so much about had turned out to be worse than a fraud. And Grant had paid the price.

Who knew what would happen to their organization now?

Max didn't really care. As long as it didn't threaten his own camp.

And he didn't think it would.

The howling of pain was clearly audible. Terry was dying. Probably very soon. A bullet to the gut would do that to a man.

Lilly stepped back into the doorway. She was almost gone, when Sadie spoke, trying to stop her.

"Where are you going, Lilly?"

"I'm going to see my dad. I don't care if he doesn't want me around. I want to be there.... he might..."

"...die?" Sadie finished the sentence for her.

"Yeah."

Sadie didn't want to still be tied up when Terry died. It might, for all she knew, be disastrous. She needed to do all she could to get out of there.

"Lilly," said Sadie. "Untie me before you go."

Lilly said nothing. But she also didn't leave.

"Come on, Lilly. This isn't fair. What if it was you? Would you like to be tied up like this?"

"No," said Lilly, still not sounding convinced.

"Then come on. Enough is enough. Get me out of here.

"OK, fine," said Lilly, finally giving in. She sounded frustrated. "But how do I do it? The knots are too tight."

"Don't you have a knife in the kitchen?"

"Yeah."

"Go get it. Hurry. Then you can go see your dad, OK?"

"OK."

In a flash, she was gone.

Sadie waited, listening to the footsteps, hoping that Lilly would return.

Finally, she was back.

"Got it," she said.

"Now be careful," said Sadie. "Make sure you're pulling the knife away from me, towards yourself. OK?"

Sadie found it a little strange that she was more component about all these sorts of everyday things, like using knives. But she didn't have much time to reflect on it, because a second later, she felt pain where before she'd felt nothing.

"Oops, sorry," muttered Lilly. "I think it's bad. You're bleeding a lot. Should I..."

There was another howl of pain from Lilly's father, Terry. It sounded bad.

"Just cut the ropes," said Sadie. "Don't worry about the cut. It's fine."

Lilly kept going, cutting Sadie one more time.

When the ropes were all off, Sadie still couldn't move. Aside from the pain she felt from the kitchen knife cuts, she couldn't feel her limbs at all.

Nor could she move them.

It wasn't just pins and needles, something she was very familiar with. But it was something like that.

Would it go away?

Probably.

Sadie couldn't see how she would lose the ability to move permanently. She'd never heard of anything like that before in her life.

Then again, she was just a kid. She hadn't had a very long life to hear about such things.

"Lilly..." Sadie started to say, but Lilly was already gone.

There was another shout of pain from outside where Terry lay. Presumably he was now surrounded by his wife and his daughter.

"Get away!" Sadie heard after a few moments. "Get her out of here!" It was Terry's voice, screaming, distorted by the intense pain he was going through. He really bellowed it, the volume extremely loud. It seemed as if Sadie could hear the death coming, just from his voice.

Sadie vaguely remembered hearing that the way he was dying was one of the most painful ways to die.

Despite her situation, Sadie cringed. She doubted Lilly would like to hear that. It was a horrible thing to hear from her father.

Why didn't he want her there?

Ever so slowly, Sadie was starting to regain feeling.

It didn't feel good, though.

It felt very bad. Very strange.

It was like the worst case of pins and needles she'd ever had. It felt like a burning sensation had run through her entire body.

It was actually painful. Almost like an itch in a way.

It was a very strange sensation.

There was another yell outside. Another scream of pain. Terry's. Who else's?

It seemed to take forever, but in the end, Sadie would guess that it took over ten minutes for her to regain the use of her limbs.

She stood up. Finally. Her legs were shaking. It felt like her blood sugar was low.

There were screams of pain coming from the front of the house.

Sadie found her way into the kitchen. There was a large kitchen knife lying on the table. Sadie grabbed it. It was about as big as her forearm.

But she was strong enough to wield it. She was strong enough to swing it, if she had to.

There was a backdoor by the kitchen.

Sadie opened it. Turned the knob. She was half expecting that someone would come from behind and stop her.

But no one did.

As she was halfway through the doorway, she turned around one last time, and she saw that Lilly had come back in.

"You're leaving?"

Lilly's face was just sadness. Sadness at losing her father. Maybe sadness at not having a friend.

"I'm leaving," said Sadie. "Sorry about your dad."

Lilly just nodded.

Sadie felt an intense sadness as she stepped through the doorway.

But as she got farther and farther away from the house, the knife still in her hand, the sadness disappeared.

It was sad about Lilly. About her dad.

But that was the way things were now.

Sadie wasn't sad that she'd lived. That she'd survived.

It'd take her a while to get back to camp, but she knew that she'd get back.

She felt foolish, having left at all. She felt even more foolish, having fallen for Terry's tricks.

She knew that she wouldn't be fooled again.

If she ran across anyone that she didn't know on the way back to the camp, she would hack at them with her kitchen knife. She'd give them hell.

Sadie was already pretty far from the house, maybe a quarter of a mile, when she realized that she had made a huge mistake.

Would Max or her mother have wanted her to walk all the way back to the camp without a gun?

No, they wouldn't. They wanted her to have a gun with her at all times.

A knife was something. But it wasn't a gun.

She hadn't gone to get her gun because it would have meant confronting Terry. It would have meant confronting death, and the pain and damage that she'd had to cause in order to survive.

But that was life now. Sadie had learned a lesson. She couldn't survive without a fight. She couldn't survive without killing. Without taking life.

And she couldn't trust strangers.

Sadie made her way back to the house. She needed that gun. She was going to get it.

She made her way around to the part of the yard where she'd shot Terry.

He was lying there, with his wife kneeling over him. His wife was singing to him in a low voice, and Terry was groaning in pain.

For some reason, Sadie knew that the sounds he was making meant that he was close to the end. Very close.

Sadie spotted her gun. It was lying close to Olivia, who had her hands on Terry's stomach. There was Terry's blood all over her hands. They were soaked in it, and Terry's clothes were completely soaked in his blood as well.

"Sweet little Terry...." Olivia was singing. "Sweet little Terry, my dear.... My darling..."

It was a strange song. The sort of song that didn't really have a tune.

And the blood provided a strange backdrop to the sound.

Sadie held the knife in her hand. She was ready to use it. She scanned the area for Lilly, but she was nowhere to be found. Probably she was cowering indoors.

Sadie knew that she'd use the knife if she had to.

But if she didn't need to, then she wouldn't.

She walked softly towards the gun, trying to make as little noise as possible.

There were a couple of tense moments, but Sadie got the gun. Her hand wrapped around the handle and she felt suddenly more confident. More secure.

"I love you, Terry," Olivia was saying. She'd stopped her song.

Terry was making choking sounds. The grunts of pain had stopped. It sounded like Terry couldn't breathe.

Sadie, meanwhile, was walking backwards. The gun was in her hand. She'd left the knife behind.

The noises Terry was making were fading. Then they stopped.

Olivia was sobbing now.

The door opened, and Sadie saw Lilly walk outside, heading towards her mother.

Lilly spotted Sadie. She turned her head.

Would Lilly give Sadie up?

No. Apparently not.

Lilly said nothing. She clearly saw Sadie, but she said nothing. Instead, she turned her head back towards her mother, and continued to walk towards her silently.

She was heading towards her dead father. About to pay her respects.

Sadie turned on her heel and started running away.

She ran until she was out of breath and her legs ached. It felt good to have her legs ache, after being immobile and unused for so long.

She would get back to the camp.

And if someone happened along the way, well, she was ready. She had her gun. It felt good in her hand, and she knew how to use it.

G eorgia had killed the man.

Somehow she hadn't died. Somehow John hadn't died.

They'd lain there, the two of them, exhausted, completely spent, after the fight, among the bodies, laughing.

It had felt strange to laugh. Strangely freeing. It was all over. For the moment. Until the next fight. Until the next random encounter with strangers that turned to violence.

It wasn't normal laughter. It wasn't exactly nervous laughter. It was instead the type of laughter that happens when you don't know what else to do, when there are no words, sayings, or facial expressions that can begin to sum up the absurdity of the situation.

Finally, Georgia had picked herself up off the ground.

John's laughter, meanwhile, had shifted back to grimaces and grunts of pain. His leg was in a bad way.

"We're going to set it when we get back to camp," said Georgia, examining the injury. "I don't want to wait around here any longer than we have to."

"You think they're all gone?"

"Only one way to find out."

"What's that?"

"Try to get on out of here. I'm going to make a sled... I'll have to drag you back."

"I can walk. Don't worry about me."

Georgia let out a little laugh. "There's no way you're walking out of here. Not on that leg."

"I'll use a stick... just get me something to walk with. I can do it. It'll be just like when I had crutches back in junior high."

"Be my guest," said Georgia. "How about this? You try that, and I'll work on my method for when yours fails."

"It's not going to fail."

Before Georgia could start getting the sledge prepared, she had to take a tour of the surrounding area. She made her way back to where they'd seen the large truck.

There was no sign of it.

The only sign that it'd been there were the dead men that it'd left behind. Georgia wondered whether the driver alone had driven off, or if there'd been other men with him.

Georgia, as a matter of habit and practicality, went through the pockets and belongings of the dead men.

There was nothing to identify them by. No wallets. No dog tags. Nothing at all that identified them in any way.

What had happened to all their stuff from before the EMP? It seemed as if someone had arranged things so that these men would not be tracked to any kind of organization.

Whatever.

Georgia didn't care.

She just wanted to get out of there. She just wanted to stay alive.

She gathered up their weapons, their knives, their

ammunition, their guns. She gathered up what she could carry of their food and she took a couple pieces of clothing to use for the sled.

Georgia used her knife to cut down some small trees nearby. They were nothing more than saplings, really. She lashed them together in a clever way with the clothes, forming a sort of inverted triangle on which she'd drag John back to the camp.

It would take a while. And it would be hard. But she'd be able to do it.

"How's that idea of yours working out, anyway?" called out Georgia, looking up from the sled she was constructing. "Those crutches going to get you back to camp?"

"Sure," shouted John, as he tried to stand up on the sticks that Georgia had tossed over to him.

He cried out in pain as he fell down.

Georgia didn't have it in her to laugh. She was too beaten down, and she was imagining the painful journey that they had back to camp in front of them.

What's more, she was thinking of her daughter.

Now, after this encounter, she felt like she was only that much further away from finding Sadie.

"Here," said Georgia, walking over to John. "Let's get you onto this thing..."

It took a little while to get John situated properly, and when he was, Georgia didn't waste any time.

It was, after all, a long way back to the camp.

25

MAX (A FEW MONTHS LATER)

I t had been a relatively calm few months. Especially considering the period that they had all gone through not so long ago, when everything had seemed so intense, as if nothing was going right, as if everything that could go wrong had gone wrong.

A lot had happened in his absence.

It had taken Max about a week to get back to the camp. His leg had hurt him as he'd walked back, but he hadn't encountered any trouble.

He'd returned to find that, in his absence, everything had apparently gone to hell.

He'd heard about how Sadie had gone missing, how Georgia had gone to look for her, and how Mandy had seemingly had pregnancy complications.

Max had felt this heart starting to skip a beat as his wife, Mandy, told him about what had happened.

"But you're OK now?" he had said, trying to hide the anxiety in his voice.

"Yeah," Mandy had said. "We don't know what it was. But everything seems to be back to normal."

Max hadn't known what to think. But there was no way to know what had happened to Mandy. Had it just been some fluke? Had it been that the baby was turned the wrong way? Something else entirely?

Max had spent a lot of his limited free time poring over the midwifery books that they had, as well as the medical encyclopedias that they'd found recently. There were a few different conditions that seemed like they might fit, but nothing was definite.

So for the months until Mandy's delivery, everyone, including Max, didn't know what to expect. They hoped for a healthy, happy baby, but they had really no way to control what would happen, except to make sure that Mandy got plenty of rest and plenty to eat.

Now it was the day everyone had been waiting for.

The day that Mandy was likely to give birth.

She had gone into labor four hours earlier.

Now, she was lying on the makeshift mattress, her legs spread apart, breathing along with Georgia's instructions.

In the little shelter, it was just Mandy, Georgia, and Max. John was limping around outside, keeping watch. He'd had a pretty good recovery from his horrible injury, but it was unlikely that he'd ever walk without a limp again. Now he had joined Max in having leg problems.

Max had tried to hold her hand, but Mandy had pulled her own hand sharply away from him, shaking her head.

"But how can I help?" said Max.

"Just keep quiet," said Mandy.

Max shot Georgia a look that said, "what am I supposed to do here?"

"Just do what she wants," said Georgia.

It seemed like wise advice, advice that Max intended to take.

Max knew he was out of his element.

Which was a strange feeling, being out of his element, since he'd been getting *into* his element since the EMP. In a strange way, the new world of violence and chaos felt more comfortable to him than the sterile, purposeless world of the office.

Over the last months, it seemed as if Max had gotten more comfortable in a variety of intense situations. They were situations that he'd never imagined that he'd be in. Before the EMP, he'd worked in an office. He'd never been in combat. He'd never been in a war.

Life since the EMP had been a war. There was no other way to put it.

The only difference between it and a regular war was that there were more enemies.

Since the EMP, almost everyone was an enemy. Everyone except those who he could trust those who had become his family.

He couldn't have done it without Georgia, without Mandy. Without everyone who'd given their lives.

For a second, he thought of Chad. An image of his face flashed into his head.

Chad had made mistakes. Big mistakes. He'd been weak in ways that a man shouldn't have been. And those weaknesses had cost him his life.

But Chad had died in an honorable way. He'd saved James's life.

Max wouldn't forget that. He knew that Georgia hadn't forgotten it. Or James. Or any of them.

"Max?" said Georgia. "You still with us?"

"Huh? Sorry," said Max, snapping back to reality.

"The water, Max?"

"Oh, yeah," said Max, feeling like he was coming out of a daze.

He got up, crossed the room, and poured a glass of water, bringing it over to Mandy. He held it for Mandy to take.

Mandy was breathing hard. Very hard. She was red in the face, and she ignored the glass of water and Max.

"For me, Max," hissed Georgia, sounding annoyed.

"Oh, sorry," said Max, getting around to the other side of the bed and handing the water to Georgia, who drank it down in a single gulp.

"We're coming in for the home stretch now," said Georgia. "You can do it, Mandy. You're going to have to push. This is going to be hard. This is going to suck. But trust me, you can do it. If I can push out those two huge kids of mine... you should have seen how big they were as babies... I know you can push out this little Max Junior..."

Mandy cried out as she started to push. He'd never seen her in so much pain.

Max took a couple of big steps back.

Seeing this scared him in some way that nothing else did. He didn't know exactly why. Maybe it was just because it was something new, something different from fighting and survival.

Or maybe it was because he was scared of bringing a new life into the world.

After all, his kid would grow up in a world that... would be radically different.

Back before the EMP, Max had never thought much about having kids. He'd figured he'd make that decision if the right woman had come along.

And she never had.

Not until the EMP.

And it turned out that she'd been living next door to

Max all that time. And they hadn't even known each other. They'd never even spoken until Max had decided to kick down her door to rescue her.

It had been a huge decision for him. Before that moment, he'd been convinced that he'd only look out for himself, that he'd die a violent death if he stopped to try to help others.

Well, he'd stopped. He'd saved Mandy.

And he was glad he had.

He doubted that he'd even be alive if he hadn't. After all, how many times had Mandy saved him? Too many to count.

Max was once again getting lost in his thoughts.

The next thing he knew, it was all over.

Mandy let out a huge grunt of pain. One final push. Strain on her face.

Georgia was reaching between Mandy's legs, grabbing something.

When she came up, she was holding a baby.

A disgusting baby, covered in all the things that a baby is covered in when it first comes into the world.

Mandy was still breathing hard, but she started to quiet down. Max looked at her and smiled. She smiled weakly back at him.

"Looks like a healthy baby... and it's a boy," said Georgia, holding him where Max and Mandy could both get a clear look at it.

It was strange looking, the baby. But only strange in the way that all newborns look strange. Their heads can seem misshapen, and their necks are almost absent. Their skin has a strange look to it.

Overall, they look funny.

And Max and Mandy's baby was no different.

It was all normal. It was a normal, healthy, soon-to-be happy baby.

"Let's name him Chad," said Max.

Georgia shot Max what might have been a quizzical, or critical, look. But she managed to stifle her normally stubborn, somewhat combative personality, and didn't say anything.

Max looked at Mandy.

"Sounds good," said Mandy, nodding.

Georgia was smiling the next time Max looked at her.

"Here you go, you hold her, Mandy," said Georgia, slowly lowering baby Chad into Mandy's eager arms. "You want to do the honors, Max?"

"The honors?"

"The umbilical cord. Sometimes the dad..."

"Oh," said Max. "Sure. Unless there's some trick to it?"

"Not really," said Georgia. "I remember how it's done. I'll show you."

"Let me go sterilize my knife," said Max, taking out his folding pocketknife, and flipping it open.

The knife had been used for many things before, but cutting an umbilical cord wasn't one of them.

All he needed was a lighter or some alcohol.

"I'll be right back with a clean knife," said Max, ducking out the door into the outdoors. As he did, he glanced back to see Mandy holding baby Chad, Georgia presiding over the whole thing.

"Is it a boy or girl?" said Sadie, suddenly popping up in front of Max. Her face was shining with excitement.

"Boy," said Max. "Help me find a lighter, will you?"

Max felt foolish. He should have been prepared for the birth. He should have had everything they might have ever needed already there.

But that's the way life was sometimes. No matter how hard you tried to prepare, things got in the way, or things cropped up unexpectantly.

* * *

READ MORE of my books here: https://www.amazon.com/Ryan-Westfield/e/B075MXJJ49

SIGN up for my newsletter to hear about my new releases. http://eepurl.com/c8UeN5

ABOUT RYAN WESTFIELD

Ryan Westfield is an author of post-apocalyptic survival thrillers. He's always had an interest in "being prepared," and spends time wondering what that really means. When he's not writing and reading, he enjoys being outdoors.

Contact Ryan at ryanwestfieldauthor@gmail.com

Made in United States
Troutdale, OR
06/18/2023

SURVIVING NEVER GETS EASY

With a child on the way, Max makes the toughest decision he's ever made. He leaves home. And now he doesn't know if he'll make it back.

Without proper medical care, Mandy hopes that she'll deliver her baby without complications.

When her daughter goes missing, Georgia must leave camp once again. She has the courage and determination to find her, but she doesn't even know which direction to head in.

Finding Shelter is book 8 of The EMP, a post-apocalyptic survival thriller series. It deals with real people fighting for their survival every inch of the way.

ISBN 9781073568079

9 781073 568079

90000